A BIRD IN THE HAND

CYNTHIA TERELST

ISBN: 978-0-648729440

 Created with Vellum

To you, all of you.
Thank you.

KEEP IN TOUCH

To be notified of future releases, and to keep up to date with other news, please join my newsletter.

https://www.subscribepage.com/p9p9yo

CHAPTER ONE

Makayla

"WAIT!"

I pulled my finger away from the lift button and turned back to Nicki and Rosanna, my two best friends. Nicki held her hand out palm down. Rosanna put her hand on top. My hand followed as it had so many times before: a tradition started at our Mathletics competitions in high school.

"May our holiday," Nicki started.

"Be full of fun," Rosanna continued.

"And learning experiences," Nicki said. I held my laughter in. As a scientist, she treated everything as a learning experience, even identity theft.

They raised their eyebrows at me expecting some sort of wisdom. "We shall be brave and step out of our comfort zones."

Our hands separated. Nicki giggled, her blonde curls bouncing, a bright pink streak standing out. "Makayla leaving her comfort zone."

OK. Here it comes. I expected nothing less from my two best friends. I faced the lift and pressed the button.

"The last time Makayla did anything unexpected was in high school," Rosanna teased.

She was probably right, but I wasn't going to tell her that. Not her, who always had perfect hair. Not her, who changed her style whenever she got bored or wanted to try something new. I was lucky to have her as a friend. She reminded me of what I could be. I told my students all the time that they could be whatever they wanted. Now I needed to start believing that myself.

The lift beeped and I entered as soon as the doors opened. Their ribbing continued as they followed me in and the lift ascended to the rooftop bar.

The text we'd received earlier said there were other people from our tour staying at the hotel and we should go mingle. And of course, Nicki and Rosanna were keen on that idea. When I stepped out of the lift, I surveyed the bar. Tall tables and chairs stood around the outside wall, the best vantage point.

"Check out the view," I said.

The sky was deepening to the navy of night. On one side, scattered lights lit up windows in the high rises. I turned and surveyed the Swan River on the other side. The city lights reflected in the water gave the impression of an enchanted upside-down city made of reds, blues, and yellows lurking under the surface.

There was an older couple, heads close together, talking. I didn't think that's who we'd be meeting. They hadn't raised their heads when the lift dinged and we stepped out. She turned her shoulder into him, suggesting she was comfortable in his presence.

At a table, three men stood watching us. They were all in shorts and buttoned shirts – smart but casual. One of them broke away and strode over. He had an easy, relaxed gait that matched his smile. Even his brown hair—messy but stylish—fit in with his relaxed persona. I was sure he was wearing some kind of fashion label I wouldn't even be able to afford to look at.

As he approached, he gazed at us one by one, making eye contact. My stomach fluttered when his hazel eyes met mine; the intimacy was penetrating. He showed great self-confidence, reminding me of Mitchell.

"Are you ladies with W.A. Adventure Tours?"

"Sure are. I'm Nicki."

"I'm Tyler."

He glanced at Rosanna, his hazel eyes intense.

"I'm Rosanna. Nice to meet you, Tyler."

"You too."

I'm sure it was nice. With her long black hair, exotic features, and constant smile, anyone would be happy to meet her. Same with Nicki—her blonde curls and friendly face were interesting and inviting. Mitchell had referred to me as 'prosaic' and that's how I preferred to be. It was his way of saying I was ordinary and lacklustre without using such blatantly negative words. My long brown hair and brown eyes had nothing distinctive about them, allowing me to hide from the spotlight.

Tyler's gaze moved to me and I was dumbstruck, like all I could focus on was his hazel eyes, and my ability to think disappeared. This was not my comfort zone. I wasn't used to the attention being on me. Usually, Mitchell would turn the attention to himself. But now I needed to speak, at least to utter my name.

"Makayla."

Tyler smiled, turned, and led us to the table. "Manny, Harrison, this is Nicki, Rosanna, and Makayla."

I gave them a half smile, enough for them to think I wasn't a stuck-up cow. This was stupid. Anyone would think I'd never met new people before. I gave my arms a shake, trying to dispel my nerves.

"Where are you from?" Manny asked. He ran his hand through his clipped brown hair.

"Sydney," Nicki said.

"We're from Melbourne," Tyler said.

"Oh no, does that mean we have to be mortal enemies?" Rosanna joked.

Tyler gave her a broad smile. He sure did smile a lot. "I prefer not to have enemies. No need to make life more complicated."

Nicki nodded in appreciation. "Love not war, right?"

"Yeah, loving is my first choice. I can make my own way in life without stepping on anyone's toes."

Fascinating. Mitchell wouldn't have had the same philosophy. According to him, climbing the ladder sometimes meant he had to climb over people, not just step on their toes. I didn't agree with it but I'd learnt not to voice my opinion.

"Mak?" Nicki said.

She was staring at me. Everyone was staring at me. Heat rose to my cheeks.

"Sorry, I missed that."

"Tyler asked if you'd like a drink."

He was studying me, waiting. I was such an idiot. I needed to stay in the present, not the past.

"Yes, please."

Tyler watched me, like he expected more. A drink choice perhaps.

"Why don't you come to the bar with me? You can choose when you get there."

I nodded. Could I act more like a social idiot? As I walked beside him to the well-stocked bar, I tried to think of something to say. I had nothing. I might as well curl into a ball like a roly poly beetle to protect any dignity I had left.

"What made you decide to holiday in Western Australia?" Tyler asked.

"It was Nicki's idea. She thought it would be good to distance ourselves from our everyday lives."

"Yeah. I get that. It feels like a different part of the world here. Do you know what people say W.A. stands for?"

I shook my head.

"Wait Awhile. From what I've seen it fits. No one is in a rush here, not like Melbourne."

"Sydney's worse. I avoid the city."

"Is this a 'mine is bigger than yours' thing?" He gave me a lopsided grin.

The bartender approached us. "What would you guys like?"

Tyler glanced at me and when I didn't speak, because somehow my new thing was to turn into a mute whenever I was put on the spot, he said, "I'll have a Moscow Mule and four beers, please."

The bartender nodded. I stared at the bottles containing different coloured liquids that glimmered in the light. Because just staring at these unknown bottles would help me decide what to drink. I rolled my eyes inwardly.

"What about you, Makayla?" Tyler prompted.

Step out of your comfort zone, Makayla.

"What's a Moscow Mule?" I asked Tyler.

"Vodka, ginger beer, and lime juice."

"I'll have one of those please."

"Alright, time for you to be converted." Tyler clapped his hands and rubbed them together.

The bartender nodded. "Put it on your tab, Ty?"

"Sure can. Thanks, Billy."

He was on a first name basis with the bartender?

"I'll bring the drinks over."

We walked back to the table in silence. Maybe Tyler thought it was easier, or that I was too weird. I wasn't usually this socially awkward. I was fine at work. I was fine in my friendship group. I could even hold conversations with strangers when I went to dinner with Mitchell and his clients or colleagues. My problem here? The intimacy of it. The way Tyler paid attention to me when I talked. The way, when Tyler looked at me, he really looked at me.

Harrison focused on us when we arrived at the table. "We were just talking about what we're looking forward to on the trip."

Tyler turned to me. My stomach clenched. Politeness was definitely his strong point. Just like earlier, he invited me to speak first. Mitchell always made it easy for me by commanding the conversation.

I really needed to stop thinking about Mitchell. It wasn't helping.

When I didn't speak, Tyler did. "Everything. Being away

from civilisation. Seeing new places. Snorkelling at Ningaloo."

The bartender arrived saving me from having to answer. He handed me my Moscow Mule. "Hope it's as good as Tyler says."

I nodded...because that was appropriate.

"What's wrong?" Nicki whispered in my ear.

"Nothing. I'm just nervous." Tyler makes me nervous.

She nodded and gave my shoulders a quick squeeze.

"Let's make a toast." Tyler raised his glass. "To new friends."

We clinked glasses. Tyler watched me as I raised the glass to my lips. The heat of the vodka was only a hint against the crispness of the ginger beer. The lime juice held the two tastes apart but at the same time pulled them together. This was a cocktail you would think nothing of drinking and then all of a sudden, wham, you'd be drunk.

"Like it?" Tyler asked.

"Very much."

"Good. Hopefully I can introduce you to more things you like."

Was he flirting with me?

By the time I was onto my third drink I felt the first touches of giddiness. My grip on my glass loosened and I joined in some of the conversation.

"You know how we're going snorkelling?" Harrison asked. He was stockier than his friends with brown hair and blue eyes.

We nodded.

"I recommend you don't do what Ty did." Harrison laughed and his blue eyes laughed with him.

Manny grinned and ran his hand through his hair. That's the second time he'd done that. Was he getting comfortable with a new cut? Or was it freshly trimmed, so it felt soft and velvety? "Show them your scar," he said to Tyler.

"I didn't know the tide was going out. With the water dropping, I got a few scrapes, and then this." Tyler lifted up his shirt. A scar, about six inches long, was etched diagonally across his stomach.

"Holy shit," Nicki said.

It was intriguing that he hadn't drawn attention to it when he'd mentioned snorkelling earlier. Was my intuition right? Did he not want to be the centre of attention? He seemed happy just being on par with everyone else. He didn't need to look better or be the best. Not like Mitchell; actually, the opposite of Mitchell.

"I didn't realise it was so bad until I got out. They had to flush the wound and check for coral fragments with tweezers."

My eyes strayed from his scar to the rest of his bared skin. Tanned, flat, toned. I wanted to touch it. The scar. I wanted to touch the scar. To see what it felt like. When I raised my eyes, Tyler's watchful gaze was on me. I blushed as if he had read my thoughts.

I wish he'd put his shirt down. It was hard to keep my eyes on his face and concentrate on what he was saying.

"Do you want to touch it?" he asked, a smirk on his face.

"No." I stepped backwards, my cheeks on fire. I wasn't putting my hands anywhere near him.

Tyler laughed. Was he making fun of me? I looked at my feet; another dead giveaway. I wanted out of there, away from him and my stupid awkwardness.

"Hey, I was only joking." His voice was soft, so only I could hear. He dropped the hem of his shirt.

I nodded. I grabbed my drink and took a gulp.

"I'm sorry. I didn't mean to make you feel uncomfortable."

He gave me a small smile. My stomach flipped. He was one of the most genuine, kind people I'd met. How I could determine that in such a short time was beyond me. Well, not really. I'd always been a people watcher. You could tell a lot about a person by how they treated others, how they acted in a group, and how they behaved when no one was watching.

And working with teenagers for eight years gave me great insight into human nature. Some kids could be nice as pie to the teachers' faces, but as soon as they turned their back, it would look like they had just sucked on a lemon sour.

I smiled in return.

"I like it when you blush. I'll have to make you do more of it."

And then he ruined it.

CHAPTER TWO

Tyler

Makayla was one of the most complicated people I'd ever met. She hardly said a word, but it was like her mind was ticking over all the time. I caught her smiling to herself more than once, like she'd thought of something funny in her head but she just wasn't confident enough to share it.

Every time I asked her to speak first or offer her opinion, her eyes widened like she was surprised I'd even asked. And then she'd stare into my eyes and I'd be adrift, as if I had been swallowed into the vault of her mind, and I'd have to remind myself where we were in the conversation. The more I watched her, the more intrigued I was.

She was wearing jeans and a short top. Sometimes she'd grab the hem of the top and pull it down if it rode too high and exposed her midriff. Was she embarrassed about her curves? I wouldn't be.

"You should hear about the new scientific technology company Ty has taken on board. They've been working on some really cool stuff," Harrison said, breaking me out of my reverie.

Everyone looked at me.

"They've developed a program to detect when children and adolescents are using technology to regulate their emotions. The program just sits in the background, monitoring, but that's not what's impressive about it. It can recognise patterns and whether technology is being overused for emotion regulation or suddenly not used at all. It has a database of different types of apps and what effect they have on emotions, good or bad." I glanced around the group. I still had their attention. Sometimes I went overboard with my enthusiasm and people disconnected.

"Wow," Nicki said. "So, it could alert parents if the algorithms detect a problem?"

"That's the plan. More and more children are suffering from anxiety and depression at younger ages. The hope is that the technology could help detect this early."

Nicki nodded. "That's remarkable. I wonder how it does that. I assume they consider different facial expressions and body language as well as time spent on the phone. Maybe they work on a micro and macro level to determine emotions."

"They could test it on you and your students, Mak. See how you compare to volatile teenagers," Rosanna said, nudging Makayla. She rolled her eyes and Rosanna laughed.

Makayla smoothed her long, shiny hair down and plaited it. Was it as silky smooth as it appeared? When the conversation changed, she took a step towards me, her soft voice held my attention while our friends continued talking amongst themselves. "I think this technology will be invaluable. Over the past eight years I've seen the impact of mental illness on students."

It was the first time she'd started a conversation all night.

"Are you a teacher?"

She shook her head. "I work with students. They have enough issues to deal with like inequality and diversity; not everyone is accepting out there in the big wide world. Being able to regulate their emotions is important, especially in times of uncertainty. Anxiety and depression hinder this."

"I've never thought about it like that. Do you deal with that much in your school?"

"All the time. I've been working closely with teachers to help them recognise the challenges students face. We have weekly meetings where I present a specific issue a student may face and we discuss how that effects their learning and their life outside of school. It's changed teacher's outlooks and even teaching practices."

"You must be proud of your work."

"I'm proud of the students. They often have doubts but they're beginning to understand how to deal with them and to be brave enough to ask the important questions."

I respected her humility and the way she helped others. Investment banking was all about deals and mergers and finding people with money to invest in people who needed money. I tried to do my best for everyone involved, and here she was, teaching the people society ignored or had nothing nice to say about, to be brave.

"Brave?"

"Did you know that, on average, male salaries are 15% higher than females? And that more women are employed in lower paid roles, such as retail, than men?"

"I've never really thought about it." Did that make me a bad person? No, not bad, maybe ignorant.

She nodded. "You wouldn't be the only one. I want the students to strive for what they want. If they want to be a receptionist, they can, whether they're male or female. If they want to be a construction manager, they can, whether they're male or female. And I want them to ask for what they're worth when they get there."

"Absolutely. Gender shouldn't stop you from living your dreams."

She tilted her head. "Are you living your dreams?"

"Mostly. I love my job. I love my family and friends. But I feel there's something missing."

Harrison approached and slung his arm around my shoulder. "What's missing?"

"The alcohol from my glass." I handed him my empty glass and then Makayla's. She smiled. Her whole face lit up, transforming her from a poised beauty to dazzling. I needed to see more of that.

The emptiness I felt inside wasn't defined. Some people would feel like this and look for love. But it wasn't like one person could fill the hole. How do you fill a hole when you don't know what caused it in the first place? And how do you define love, anyway? I had plenty of love from those close to me. Was one type of love more important than another? I didn't need a person to help me feel complete. I was a well-rounded, well-adjusted male. Having a relationship wouldn't change that or improve it, would it?

Working on this latest project gave me a sense of fulfillment. Like I was doing something worthwhile. Maybe that was something I needed to pursue.

Makayla's attention moved from me to the other conversation. They were debating whether tacos or nachos were better. Where had that conversation even come from? Makayla listened but didn't contribute. When I saw her nodding about how corn chips were an ideal dinner food, I decided to help her join the conversation. She didn't really need my help. She was capable, but giving her a nudge wouldn't hurt.

"Nachos?" I asked her.

She nodded. I grabbed her hand and raised it into the air. "Team Moscow Mule vote for nachos."

I grinned at her wide eyes.

"You can't just corrupt Mak with your hot body and cute smile," Nicki said, her hands on her hips.

Makayla yanked our hands down.

"Excuse me, Makayla corrupted me."

She wrenched her hand away.

Rosanna laughed. "In your dreams, lover boy."

"Dreams can come true."

"And what exactly are you dreaming about?" Nicki asked, a twinkle in her eyes.

Makayla stepped away from me.

"Nachos, of course." I gave her a wink. She gave me a death stare.

CHAPTER THREE

Makayla

I PUSHED my suitcase into the lift, excited for the start of our big adventure. My stomach squeezed when I thought of Tyler's smile. It was warm and open. But was it true? Mitchell's wasn't always. Why was I even thinking about it anyway?

The way Tyler joked about me corrupting him had set me on edge. That was never going to happen in any shape or form. Not him corrupting me. Or me corrupting him. And there was no dream where he, with his so-called hot body, impeccable wardrobe, and cute smile, ended up with *me*. Nor did I want him to.

I'd never strayed from the life I'd planned out. Since I'd met Mitchell eleven years ago, I knew where I wanted my life to head and all decisions I'd made since then were in pursuit of that dream. All decisions, that was, until Mitchell decided he no longer had the same vision and had broken up with me six months ago. For ten years I'd given everything to that dream, that man.

The lift dinged and the doors opened on the ground floor. I followed Nicki and Rosanna out.

"You better not be thinking about him," Nicki said, raising her eyebrows at me, her tone stern.

How did she know?

"This holiday is a Mitchell free zone," Rosanna added. "Every time you mention him, think about him—"

"Talk like him—"

"Act like him—"

"You'll need to choose a deed from the deed jar."

I stopped in my tracks. "The what?"

"Well, it's not a literal jar. It's a list on my phone," Rosanna said.

They continued walking to the front doors.

"What sort of list?" I followed them, catching up, the wheels of my suitcase gliding easily across the marble floor.

"Hopefully you won't need to find out." Nicki smirked.

This was not good. Not in the slightest. They'd been telling me for the past three months that my grieving time was over. Only three months was acceptable. That I needed to forget the past and embrace the future and all it could be. I understood what they were saying but ten years was a lot to let go of.

I didn't think I wanted to go back to Mitchell. The more time I spent apart from him the more I realised he wasn't such a great person. The thing was, my dream had been so close I could almost touch it. We'd saved enough money for a substantial deposit on a house, and not even a house in a shitty suburb. A good suburb where crime was low and families were bright and cheerful. Somewhere where futures were made.

We stepped out into the warm Perth air. A small bus was waiting for us, *W.A. Adventure Tours* plastered on the side in wild pink writing. A sticker of a sulphur-crested cockatoo in a mankini, blowing kisses, was the focal point. I narrowed my eyes. First the suggestion that we should *mingle* with other guests and now this. Was this some sort of singles bus tour?

One look at the man standing beside the bus and my feet slowed. His short-sleeved shirt was unbuttoned half way down his chest. A gold chain rested against his bronze skin. He licked his lips as he looked us up and down, his gaze lingering.

"Ladies," he drawled. "Is there a Nicki amongst you?"

Nicki stepped forward; her curls tied back in a ponytail. She held out her hand. "That's me."

"It's a pleasure to meet you." His mouth lifted on one side as he turned his attention to Rosanna and me. My throat constricted. "And you ladies, too. I'm Frank."

I gave a fake smile. That's all I could manage as I handed my suitcase over for him to put in the trailer. This was stepping out of my comfort zone all right.

I followed Nicki and Rosanna to the front door and onto the bus. A wolf whistle broke the air. I cringed. Wolf whistling was distasteful and should be reserved for creeps in movies only.

"Ooh, we have some pretty ones here."

I turned towards the sound and found a white cockatoo perched behind the driver, bobbing up and down, in a mankini.

"Pretty ones. Pretty Girls. Pretty girls for the pretty boys," it squawked.

Laughter. The bus driver grinned at us. Nicki approached the bird. She stopped in front of it and bent down, her face close, blocking our view.

"Who's a pretty cocky?" she said to him.

"I'm a fucking pretty boy."

Laughter again.

"Well, yes you are." Nicki stood back and glanced at us, her face lighting up with a smile and laughter on her lips. "You're a funny bird. What's your name?"

"Cock Monster."

Who the hell would call a bird that?

The driver nodded. "It's true."

Could this really be happening? Singles bus? Foul-mouthed cockatoo?

Comfort zone.

Smile. Just smile.

I followed Nicki down the aisle, not looking at any of the other passengers. I didn't want any of them to think I wanted to hook up. I shook my head. Looking at someone didn't mean anything. Anyway, they'd be more drawn to Nicki or Rosanna than plain old me.

When we reached an empty row, we filed in. I looked at the seats behind us and found Manny, Harrison and Tyler. People I knew and at least felt comfortable with. Well, mostly.

Tyler was looking at me with that same intensity he had last night. My stomach fluttered. I diverted my eyes and took my seat. That man was an enigma—serious one minute, a jokester the next. I swear he'd gotten great pleasure from making me blush. And even worse, he was good at it. Problem was I couldn't even stay angry with him because I didn't believe there was any malice behind it.

"Good morning, Moscow Mule Partner," Tyler said.

CHAPTER FOUR

Tyler

MAKAYLA SMILED A FRACTION TOO LATE.

"That cocky is hilarious," Manny said.

I nodded, laughing with him and Harrison. The cockatoo fed off the passengers' laughter and laughed and danced in response, flapping its wings. Its yellow crest stood upright.

"Welcome aboard, ladies," the bus driver said. "Our first stop will be Cottesloe Beach where we will enjoy fish and chips. Then we'll drive to The Pinnacles to check into our hotel before enjoying the magnificent sunset over the desert."

The guide hopped on the bus and the doors closed behind him. "Then our adventure begins. We'll drop you in the middle of the desert." He paused. "Give you some lessons about stars and navigation and then we'll leave you to find your way to the target."

He gazed at each of the twenty passengers on board, smiling to himself, as if he were measuring us up. Makayla, Nicki and Rosanna chatted amongst themselves.

"You didn't tell me this was a singles bus tour," Makayla accused her friends.

"It's not a singles bus tour," Nicki replied. She was right. Two of the couples we'd met already were married and there was at least one other couple on the bus from what I could tell. And Manny was definitely a taken man.

"Really? What's with the cockatoo then? With the pretty girls for pretty boys."

I tried to keep my laughter in. That was one foul mouthed bird. It lived up to its name. Nicki caught me listening and gave me a wink. I should have looked away and made an effort not to eavesdrop, but there was no point when I'd already been sprung.

"It probably says that to everyone," Rosanna said. "You know, to break the ice."

"Lighten up, Makayla. You're single. The bird's single. Tyler's single."

What the hell? There was no need to bring me into it. I may have found Makayla interesting, but I was not *interested* in her. I had no time or energy for a relationship or fling or anything that involved the opposite sex. Makayla looked at me wide eyed while Nicki and Rosanna laughed.

"And Frank? He sets the tone for this whole bus," Makayla said.

I clenched my jaw. He must have undressed them with his eyes, too; it had made me recoil. Like owner, like bird. Both pervs.

"Oh yeah, he was gross," Rosanna said. "Like one of those sleaze buckets in nightclubs who rub up against girls."

"If he's not the epitome of a singles bus I don't know what is." Makayla crossed her arms.

I watched Nicki roll her eyes through the cracks of the seats. "Let me put it this way, neither the bird nor Frank were mentioned on the website."

"I'm not sure I believe you."

Frank clapped his hands to get our attention. "Now, to get ourselves acquainted, I'd like each of you to stand up, one at a time. Tell us your name, where you're from, and an interesting fact."

I groaned inwardly. Give me a boardroom, clients, merger presentations, and I was at home. Leading my team, giving direction, driving motivation, that was my life. But ask me to tell a bunch of strangers an interesting fact about myself and I was lost. What was I going to say? Talking about my job would be lame. When had work become the only thing that defined me?

I listened as the people up front gave their introductions row by row. One lady had been a surrogate for her sister, which was impressive. One guy had sky dived naked. What would compel someone to do that? To have their junk flying around in the wind?

Then it was the row in front of us. Rosanna stood up. "I'm Rosanna. I was going to be a professional dancer before I broke my leg."

Nicki and Makayla looked at each other and shared some private joke. Rosanna gave them both a hard stare. It was epic, but probably had the opposite effect to what she wanted, when they both cracked up laughing. Laughter sounded good on Makayla.

Nicki stood up, twirling her bright pink streak of hair in her fingers. That streak was so bright it reminded me of dragon fruit. When my sister was young, we teased her by telling her we were eating dragon eggs. She was mortified.

"I'm Nicki, from Sydney. I'm a microbiologist. I study small things under a microscope."

"She's talking about your ..." Harrison said, looking at my groin. Seriously anyone would think he was fifteen not thirty-three.

"Maybe she's talking about your brain," I said.

If the thought of getting up in front of all these people was bad for me, it would be worse for Makayla. She'd been nervous enough yesterday to last a lifetime. When it was her turn, she stood up and gazed around the bus. Her loose hair was now plaited. I watched her closely. The confidence I saw was not what I'd expected. But was she confident? She didn't make eye contact with anyone until she got to me. I was entranced by those brown eyes, so deep and enticing, like rich molten chocolate. I had to force myself to listen or I wouldn't have heard a word.

"Hi, I'm Makayla Dawson from Sydney. My favourite book is *Diary of a Wombat*."

She was a Dawson, like me, but that's not what piqued my interest. It was the title of her favourite book: *Diary of a Wombat*. What was that? If I hadn't heard their previous conversation, I would have thought that was a euphemism for wombats—eats, roots and leaves. We used to say that phrase when referring to hook-ups. But there was no way she would refer to anything sexual. Just mere flirting embarrassed her.

The small smile returned and she sat. Manny and Harrison looked at me. That was my cue. I stood up. Time to turn on the charm, if that's what you called it. I smiled broadly. My old mentor's voice echoed in my head: 'Believe in what you're selling'.

"Hi, I'm Tyler from Melbourne." My eyes stopped on Makayla for a moment before drifting to Nicki. "I'm not a microbiologist but I've been intimate before with a pair of tweezers." Taking a prompt from Harrison's earlier comment, I focused on Makayla to make sure I had her attention, before looking down...at my feet. Then I dropped my voice and said directly to her, "I guess that's not the best thing to share on a *singles* bus."

Nicki and Rosanna laughed. Makayla blushed and snapped her head around, and that made them laugh even more. I couldn't believe I could make her blush on cue...every single time. She wasn't that innocent if she got my joke about tweezers and the size of my penis. She didn't appear to be upset. If she did, I would have stopped straight away.

We continued the introductions and then chatted amongst ourselves until the bus pulled into a carpark. A stunning view greeted us from the window. Terraced lawns spread to a beach with startling white sand, so white it almost hurt my eyes. Beyond that was water so clear and azure blue it appeared enchanted. I pulled my Ray-Bans down, shielding my eyes from the brightness.

Frank stood up.

"Tables have been set up for us on the bottom terrace." The bus door slid open. "Head on down. Fish and chips will be delivered soon."

Manny, Harrison and I followed Makayla, Rosanna and Nicki to the tables positioned perpendicular to the beach so we could all enjoy the view. The beach stretched around in a curve and in the middle of it, almost on the sand itself, was a grand two-storey building. It had old world arches and matching arched windows—the Indiana Teahouse, one of the most photographed buildings in Perth.

"The view is amazing," Nicki said as she sat. Makayla and Rosanna sat beside her. We took the seats opposite.

"You wouldn't believe that type of blue existed unless you were here," Manny said.

"It's not really blue," Nicki said. "The water absorbs long wavelength light like red, orange and yellow and short wavelength light like blue and violet are scattered, making the water look blue."

"Cool. I never knew that," Harrison said.

"Ladies and gents, there are coolers at the end of your tables. Beer and wine are your choices." Frank smiled around at the group.

I gave Makayla a smile. "Shame, no Moscow Mules for us." I stood up and handed out the drinks.

"Rosanna, what type of dancing do you do?" Harrison asked.

She sat up straight, her jet-black hair shining in the sun. Her friends looked at her expectantly, hints of smiles on their faces.

"Oh, I don't dance anymore."

"That must have been hard to have your dream ripped away like that because of a broken leg."

Rosanna shifted in her seat. A giggle escaped Nicki's lips. Makayla laughed long and hard. I needed more of that like I needed more of her smile. It spread a lightness through me.

"Rosanna was a pole dancer," Nicki said, trying to compose herself.

"Well, I guess we all have different dreams." Manny took a gulp of his beer.

Rosanna turned to her friends, scrunching up her face. "Not a pole dancer as in a stripper. A pole dancer as in the artistic type."

"Yeah, and not a professional as in a professional," Nicki said. The blonde curls that had escaped her ponytail bounced as she laughed. "A professional, as in I better try to get a job as a dancer seeing my parents paid so much to develop my *talent.*"

"To be honest, the broken leg was probably a blessing," Rosanna said. "It gave me a legitimate reason not to pursue dancing."

"How about you, Makayla, are you living out your dream on this singles bus tour?" I asked, expecting her to blush at the mention of it.

Her eyes narrowed before a smug smile appeared. Looking directly at me, she said, "To be honest, I'm disappointed so far. The pickings are slim."

Manny let out a roar of laughter and slapped me on the back. "Burn."

CHAPTER FIVE

Makayla

Nicki, Rosanna and I walked along the water's edge. The remnants of waves swept over our feet, cool but not unpleasant. The silence was broken by seagulls squawking their hellos and the squeals of children playing or making sandcastles. It felt like we stepped into a time warp instead of the other side of the country. It was true what Tyler had said, things moved at a different pace here, a different level. Slower. Muted. Allowing someone time to just be. To exist in a world where just existing was frowned upon, where you were expected to be present, to be effective, to do more.

Tyler. What on Earth had made me speak back to him like that? Telling him he was slim pickings? Anyone with an X chromosome would say he was the hottest guy on the bus. I guess they could be right. Everything about him was...nice. Nice to look at. Nice to speak to. Nice to be around. But his insistent teasing about it being a singles bus when he knew damn well it wasn't made me grit my teeth.

"I'm glad there are some fun people on the tour," Nicki said.

"I know. The guys are great. At least they have a sense of humour, and can hold a conversation about something other than sport." Rosanna glanced back at them.

"Tyler's funny," Nicki said.

"Not really," I replied. "More like annoying."

"You're just pissed that he was teasing you," Nicki said.

And he did that perfectly, more than once. Mitchell wouldn't have done that. Not tease me in front of a crowd. That would be below him. Teasing and having a light-hearted good time were not things you would associate with Mitchell. And every time that Tyler teased me, he would get a rise out of me. It seemed like he enjoyed it.

"Mak." Nicki's hard voice caught me by surprise.

"What?"

"You were thinking about M." Her frown morphed into an evil grin. I remembered their threat from earlier.

"No, I wasn't."

"You were."

What was I going to say? That I was thinking about Tyler? That would be so much worse. They would never let up about it. I couldn't deny thinking about one without admitting I was thinking about the other. I stayed silent.

"Rosanna, get your phone out. We need to give Mak a deed."

"This is stupid. I'm not doing a deed." I walked faster, trying to get away. But I'd reached the end of the beach and had no choice but to turn around and walk right into them. I picked up speed again, even though there was no point. I was trapped. They would catch up to me when we got back to the bus and then they would make sure this wasn't just a quiet game. They would make sure others heard of it. The thought of Tyler having something else to tease me about was enough to make me slow down.

"You have no choice. It's two against one," Rosanna said. The glee in her voice was disconcerting. "Pick a number between one and thirty."

"You have thirty options?" Geez, they had no confidence in me.

"We hoped that you would learn quick," Rosanna said.

"We do have reserve deeds, just in case."

I shook my head. It's not like I thought about Mitchell all the time. Or spoke about him all the time. In fact, I thought I had gotten better over the past few months. At first, when I moved into my unit, I'd missed him like crazy. It was like I had no purpose when I didn't have someone to serve. And having no dream or goal to work towards was unsettling. When I closed my eyes, I could still see the perfect house on a quiet street. I could picture me sitting on a porch swing watching our children play hopscotch on the driveway. They'd call me over to join their game, full of smiles and laughter.

"Pick a number," Rosanna said, giving me a nudge.

"Fine. Six."

The two of them stopped and glanced at the phone, then at each other and then at me. Rosanna grinned.

"You need to go up to the person you like least and start a conversation with him or her."

Nicki clapped her hands like a school child. "Oh, it's definitely a him—Tyler."

There was no way I was having a conversation with Tyler while they watched. But that was unfair, we had talked to each other last night and he'd been pleasant, mostly. I didn't dislike him. How could you dislike someone who was so nice? Well, nice but annoying.

The only other option was Frank. He gave me the creeps but maybe I'd read him wrong. Tyler might have been annoying, like a punch in the face annoying, because he was always there and nice and just...But he didn't make me feel uncomfortable the way Frank did. But to have to speak to him, actually approach him and speak to him, I don't know. I didn't want him to think I was into him or anything.

"I might speak to Frank."

Rosanna and Nicki raised their eyebrows at each other.

"You have twenty-four hours to complete the deed."

WE FILED off the bus into the hotel carpark. The buildings were on the older side—red bricks and mission brown paint—but were well maintained. The garden was neat, filled with spring flowers. The driver started pulling our suitcases out of the trailer.

"OK. When I call your name, come forward and collect your keys and suitcases," Frank said.

We stood together in our friendship groups waiting for our names to be called. The cocky perched on top of the open bus door throwing squawks and words out into the afternoon air. Its white feathers bright in the afternoon sun.

"Aren't you afraid the cocky will fly away?" Nicki asked Frank.

"No, he's scared of heights."

I tilted my head. Was he serious?

Frank considered his clipboard. "Nicki, Rosanna, you're in room twelve."

I looked at my friends. Why weren't we together?

"Makayla and Tyler, you're in room ten."

Shivers spread through my body and I latched onto Nicki's arm. Breathe. Words. Use your words. "I'm sorry, there must be some kind of mistake."

Frank glanced at us and then back at his paper. "No. That's what it says. Makayla and Tyler Dawson, room ten."

What fresh hell was this? I glanced at Tyler. They could not seriously expect me to share a room with him. Or any man for that matter. The frown Tyler wore matched the one I'm sure was on my face.

"It's OK. We'll clear it up," Rosanna said. "Let him finish and then we'll speak to him."

I nodded. What else was there to do?

I hadn't shared a space with any other male except for Mitchell. Even when I chaperoned on school camps, the female teachers shared with females and males with males. I felt unsteady at the prospect. Like all my bones and organs had pushed to one side trying to escape from him and I was about to fall over. I shook my head at the ridiculous notion. I took a deep breath to recentre myself.

When all the other passengers left for their room, we approached Frank. Tyler and his friends followed.

"Frank, there must be a mix up with the room," I said.

"Tyler and Makayla didn't meet until yesterday," Rosanna said.

Frank considered us and turned to Craig, the driver, who shrugged. "I thought they were married, what with the last name."

"Maybe I can bunk in with Harrison and Manny," Tyler suggested. "Or maybe there is a spare room we could have."

I unclenched my teeth. At least Tyler was taking this seriously and wasn't treating it like some sort of joke.

"We'll go speak to the manager," Frank said.

I hoped they could find a solution. But what if they couldn't? I couldn't ask one of the other girls to swap with me, that wouldn't be fair. Them sharing a room with someone they didn't know would be the same as me doing it. It could be worse; it could be Frank I was sharing a room with. Oh God, I wouldn't have to share a bed, would I?

Frank's mouth was tight when he returned. "Sorry, they're fully booked. I asked if we could move a bed in with Harrison and Manny but they said fire regulations wouldn't allow it."

I took a deep breath. We were both adults. It wouldn't be the first time strangers had to share a room. There was no point making a scene out of it. It would put a dampener on everyone's night and I didn't want to be responsible for that.

"It's OK. We'll be fine."

Frank nodded, grabbed his bag and headed off to his room...just like that. Like he didn't even care. You would have thought he'd try a bit harder. Maybe look at other hotels or offer to give up his own room. But no, he was just dismissive. I wanted to give his retreating back the finger.

The cocky squawked at us in glee, so loud anyone in the carpark, and even the closest rooms, would be able to hear it. "Oooh, nooky nooky."

Heat rose in my cheeks. I glared at the damn bird and then at Tyler. He just shrugged. Everyone burst out laughing and started to talk at once.

"The look on Mak's face was—"

"It matched Tyler's. I've never seen him look so horrified—"

"Maybe once. Remember when he had to buy Clarissa tampons but he didn't know about sizes."

"Oh yeah."

"Mak, can you do the face again?"

I gave them all the finger as I collected my case.

"Tyler, how are you going to cope? When was the last time you spent the night with a woman?"

Male laughter followed me.

"He might die if he tries anything," Rosanna said. "She's so tense."

"Yeah, ready to explode. Like a bottle of coke just waiting for a mentos," Nicki said.

I kept walking. Footsteps followed. I snuck a peak. It was Tyler. The others' laughter and words started to fade.

"A huge eruption."

"From Makayla or Tyler?"

"From the nooky nooky."

Roars of laughter. I shook my head. They were worse than the teens I worked with. I know they were only trying to lighten the situation, but seriously, did they have to bring the nooky nooky into it? That stupid bird.

I hadn't missed the part where Manny said Tyler hadn't spent the night with a woman for a while. Was he one of those guys who got his fill and left? Maybe. He seemed to be a carefree kind of guy, maybe he didn't take females or sex seriously? I, on the other hand, did. He had better not get any ideas.

The last thing I heard was one of the girls calling out, "Maybe you can finish the deed, Mak."

CHAPTER SIX

Tyler

MAKAYLA OPENED the door and my stomach dropped. I was hoping there would be a couch or something I could sleep on. No such luck. Just one bed for us to share. Of course, there would be, we *were* a married couple after all. Thank goodness it was a queen. That was one thing to be grateful for. At least we wouldn't be sleeping on top of each other.

Makayla flexed the fingers on her free hand. I doubt anyone would have seen that emotional betrayal. She kept it all hidden inside. Why?

I rolled my case in after Makayla. We had an hour to kill before we returned to the bus. Dumping my case and escaping to the guy's room would be rude. Besides, Makayla and I had gotten along alright last night. I was sure we would be fine.

I looked around the space. There was a small table with two chairs and the bed. If I sat on the bed, would that send the wrong message? What message did I want to send—relaxed, friendly? This was stupid. I was a grown arse man. I didn't want Makayla to feel uncomfortable but I didn't need to second guess myself. I walked to the bathroom and peeked in. It was dated, but clean and functional. Notes of lemon blossom filled the air. Clarissa had always referred to it as the smell of happiness. It was one of her favourite candle scents and she still enjoyed it to this day.

"I'm going to have a shower before we go. It will probably be too late when we get back," I said.

Makayla nodded. "Good idea."

"Do you want to go first?"

"Sure. Thanks."

She laid her suitcase down and opened it. I tried not to look at the contents but she was right in front of me. I was expecting everything to be compartmentalised, organised and structured like she was. And I wasn't disappointed. It may have not been as neat as say, an army sergeant's, but everything was perfectly folded and seemed to have its place. She pulled out a toiletry bag and some clothes and headed to the bathroom.

Sitting on the bed I let out a sigh. It was a weird situation to be in. The guys weren't wrong when they said I hadn't spent the night with a woman in a long time. It's not that I didn't like women's company. I spent a lot of time with my sister and I enjoyed that time. I just didn't have the bandwidth. And couldn't find the right person. And didn't like the singles' scene. I liked the way my life was. Uncomplicated. And women always complicated everything. And a woman like Makayla would be the most complicated of all.

The water started in the shower. I imagined Makayla stepping in, her brown hair loose and cascading down her back, and the water flowing over her curves. All of her curves. Her nakedness. Was her whole body as tanned as her arms and legs?

What the hell? That was not something I should be thinking about. Abort mission.

I grabbed the TV remote off the bedside table. TV would be a good, easy distraction. I flicked through the channels. Flick. Pause. The quicker I flicked, the more it kept my mind off Makayla in the shower. After what seemed like forever Makayla opened the door and came out. I glanced at my watch—forty-five minutes she'd been in there. It may as well have been forever. There was only fifteen minutes left for me to get ready. Another perfect example of why I didn't need a woman in my life.

AS WE DROVE through the desert I couldn't take my eyes off the hundreds, maybe thousands, of limestone pillars of all shapes and sizes. They protruded from the golden-orange sand as if they were in a gathering, listening to sacred wisdom. People walked among them; some pillars towered above their heads, others barely reached their waist. When we changed direction, the positioning of the sunlight changed. The pinnacles went from being a part of the desert itself—orange and blending in—to growing darker as if harbouring secrets.

"The Aborigines used this place for women's business," Frank said. "They would come here for ceremonies and to give birth."

"How were the pinnacles formed?" someone from the front of the bus asked.

"One Dreamtime story states that when men tried to reach this sacred place, the gods punished them by burying them alive. The pinnacles are their fingertips coming out of the sand."

Goes to show you shouldn't defy the gods.

I expected Nicki to give us a scientific explanation but her eyes were transfixed on the scene surrounding us. As were Makayla's and Rosanna's.

"We'll let you out here so you can enjoy the sunset from the viewing platform. After that, we'll drive further into the desert to start our navigation experience."

The yellow desert was dotted with green shrubs, beyond that were white sand dunes and the magnificent royal blue of the ocean. The golden glow of the setting sun swathed light and shadow across the desert landscape. The shadows cast by the pinnacles became longer as darkness descended. Then only silhouettes were left as the orange glow of the sky changed to blackness and the stars emerged.

We hopped back onto the bus, talking in hushed tones. It didn't feel right to talk about what we had just witnessed. It was like a part of my soul, hidden before, had been touched.

"Your roommate will be your team mate for the navigation by the stars challenge," Frank said. Makayla's shoulders didn't slump like I expected them to. Thank goodness for that. "You'll all start at the same place and will need to navigate your way to three different points. Your next clue will be found at each of these points. When you reach each point, you need to radio in with the UHF radios I will hand out when you get off the bus."

When we got off the bus, I was thankful for the head-lights. Beyond their reach was blackness. Frank passed out torches to each person, not to be used for the navigation but for reading the clues, and one two-way and compass for each pair. Then he gave us our first instructions on a piece of paper.

"Don't read that yet. I need to give you a lesson on navigating using the Southern Cross and using the compass. The compass will be your back up." Frank looked up to the sky and we all followed suit. Makayla and I stood close together, bumping into each other. I steadied myself and then turned my attention to the sky. The headlights turned off and the blackness beyond was transformed. I sucked a breath in. I'd seen plenty of stars before in the city and country. The city lights always made stars look pale but, in the country, stars were as bright as could be. As children, when we went camping, it had been hard to choose the brightest one to wish upon. This, though, was next level. The band of stars, clustered together, drew my eye—a cloud of them with a pink tinge. The Milky Way.

"Can you all see the Southern Cross?"

I studied the sky and found the four bright stars that formed the cross with the fifth, duller star, keeping them company. When I was little, I sometimes got mixed up and found a different four stars, but my dad taught me to look for that fifth one, so I would know I had the right constellation. I wasn't sure if Makayla had found it so I pointed it out to her. She nodded.

"Above the Southern Cross, you will see the pointer stars from Centaurus." Frank waited until satisfied we all saw it. "Now, if you draw a line through the cross from head to foot and then find the spot in the middle of the two pointers and draw a line from there, where those two lines meet is the

South Celestial Pole. Draw a line straight down from that, to the horizon, and you have found south."

Hands and fingers went everywhere as we figured out where south was. Then we were shown how to use the compass.

"Good. Good. Now split off in your pairs. I'll make sure one last time that you've got it right, then you can head off."

Makayla and I separated from the group and waited for Frank.

"The proper name for the Southern Cross is Crux," I said, breaking the silence. "In ancient times it could also be seen in the northern hemisphere."

"But not now?" Makayla asked, turning to me. Light and shadow highlighted the planes of her face. I bet she had no idea how beautiful she was.

"No, the Earth's axis has changed."

"And it will keep changing, like everything else. Nothing stays constant." She had a sad tone to her voice.

"The stars stay constant."

"Until they explode."

CHAPTER SEVEN

Makayla

I HELD the instructions in my hand. The starlight was bright but not bright enough to read. Tyler switched his torch on so we could read together. *Five hundred metres due south. One hundred metres due west. Fifty metres due south.*

"OK. Generally, it's 1.3 steps per metre," Tyler said, turning his torch off.

Was that right? I had no idea. "How do you know that?"

"Sometimes my dad took us out camping and would set a scavenger hunt course for us."

"He let kids wander in the bush?"

Even in the near darkness I could see Tyler's jaw clench. "We knew bushcraft. We weren't stupid kids who would wander aimlessly."

"Yeah. OK. That makes sense." I'd obviously hit a sore spot. I wasn't sure which part was so offensive.

My voice would have had something to do with it. Stupid. I was usually more careful in my delivery. Ever since our last

Mathletics competition I'd curbed what I'd said. I'd learnt the consequences of rash words that day. It wasn't the fact that I'd pointed out a problem. It was the way I'd said it. And then there was Mitchell.

"We need to head south for 650 steps," Tyler said, his voice serious. The lightness, the teasing tone I always expected was gone. "Let's find south and head off."

Our feet moved over the sand as we counted our first one hundred steps to ourselves. The sand was crusty in some parts, making walking easy, and soft in others. Each time we hit a soft spot walking was more difficult as we had to lift our feet higher. When we reached each one-hundred-step increment we said it out loud to each other.

Voices drifted across the desert reminding me that we weren't alone. No one had announced over the radio that they had found their first destination point. When we reached it would it stand out? Or would it have a motion sensor and light up when we were within a metre of it? How would we know when we found it?

"Six hundred," Tyler said.

"Yep."

I'd lost count. Or rather I'd forgotten about counting. I wasn't going to tell Tyler that. I didn't want the lecture or condescending comments. I didn't want to hear about how I let my mind wander and that sort of behaviour would lead us to fail. I didn't want to hear how he should be in charge.

"Team two have secured their location," a voice said over the radio.

I picked up my pace. I didn't want to be the last. Tyler kept up with me easily. I counted to fifty in my head, determined not to lose count this time.

"OK. One hundred metres west now," I said. I didn't wait for Tyler to agree or disagree, I just checked out the stars, found west and headed off. I expected Tyler to be right by my side but he fell in behind me. He did the same at the next direction change. When we reached our destination, I scanned the ground with my torch to find our next clue. A little green flag with the number four on it protruded from the sand. I rushed over to it. We weren't the last.

Tyler clicked the button on the two-way. "Team four have found their next clue."

I pulled the flag out of the ground and unfurled the instructions attached to it. North west was where we needed to head first. I found our direction.

Tyler sighed. "This is supposed it be a team effort."

Where had that come from? We were walking as a team. Changing direction as a team.

"It is."

"Really? In investment banking, team effort means we stop and consult at each step."

Why? So he could take over? I started walking. Tyler said nothing and followed.

"Perhaps you can at least tell me how many steps we have to take so if you lose count again, I can cover our arses."

"I didn't lose count."

"Are you sure about that?"

I rolled my eyes and walked faster. He didn't know what he was talking about. I kept walking, keeping him out of my head and the number of steps in it until I reached 260.

Then I found the next direction. "We need to go west." I pointed west. "Would you like to consult and check my direction?"

Tyler sighed. I'd never met a man who sighed so much. I didn't know what his problem was, I'd consulted with him just like he'd asked me to.

"How far?"

"Three hundred metres."

I set off again, counting my steps. We were half way there when he said, "It would probably be a good idea to stop every now and then to check we are still going in the right direction."

"We are."

"The desert is a big place. Sometimes you can get disorientated."

"I'm not disorientated."

What gave him the right to question me?

"It would only take a few seconds and we could be sure."

"I *am* sure. I don't need you mansplaining to me."

"Ok. Just saying."

"Will you shut up? I'm trying to count."

"Yes, ma'am."

I clenched my teeth. Who the hell did he think he was? 'Let's stop and re-evaluate'. I knew exactly where I was going and I didn't need him to tell me otherwise. He was just like Mitchell. Once, I was putting together a bookshelf from IKEA and was figuring out which screws were the right length. He huffed and took over, like I couldn't even get screws right. I ignored Tyler and changed direction according to the instructions I'd memorised and stormed off.

Another change in direction later we'd arrived at our next target. I switched on the torch and scanned the sand. I couldn't see anything. Tyler stood still and I walked circles around him. Where was it? It had to be here. Maybe I wasn't looking for a flag. Maybe it was something else. Other teams started to call in. My torch sweeps became more erratic.

"Are you sure you read the instructions right?" Tyler asked.

"I read them perfectly fine, thanks."

"So, we needed to go 300 metres north-west, 200 metres west and 300 metres north-west?"

"Yes. Isn't that what we did?"

His mouth twisted.

"Well?" I asked, stopping in front of him and pulling myself up to my full height.

He shrugged.

"If you've got something to say, say it."

"Some of the directions we were heading in were questionable."

"What do you mean?"

"Well, that north-west stint started off that way but ended up more like west."

"No, it didn't."

"Yes, it did. Right about the time I said we should check."

I ignored him and started to look again. It had to be here. All the teams had checked in except for us.

"Maybe you could actually show me the instructions," he said, holding out his hand.

I had shown them to him, hadn't I? My mouth went dry. Rude. That was rude. I was rude. I swallowed the lump in my throat but couldn't utter a word. I'd acted like such a dick, and he'd done nothing to deserve that. I kept my eyes averted, and tried to keep my hand from shaking as I handed the instructions over.

He read them and handed them back. "I think you read them wrong."

I stared at the piece of paper in my hand. My stomach dropped, like a student realising they'd studied for the wrong exam. The last instruction said north, north-west. Heat rushed to my face. What an idiot. I was so pigheaded that I'd ruined the whole night.

"Team Four, what's your status?" Frank called over the radio.

Tyler raised the radio to his mouth. Now the whole bus would hear how I'd stuffed up. "We seem to have taken a wrong turn."

"Do you need us to pick you up?"

"No. I think we will try to strategise it out first."

"Ten-four."

Tyler lowered the radio and looked at me. "What do you want to do?"

Going back fifteen minutes in time wasn't an option. If it was, I could have found my manners. And maybe put some effort into team work.

"I don't know. What do you think?"

I snuck a look at Tyler. He wasn't scowling or glaring at me. He gazed around our surroundings biting his bottom lip. Mitchell would not have been like this. He would have let everyone know it was my fault, and even if it wasn't he would have twisted it so it was.

"I'm sorry, Tyler."

He nodded. That was probably the best I could ask for after what I'd done. I looked at the ground, fidgeting with the hem of my top. He stood quiet, a furrow between his eyebrows as he thought. "We could try to back track, but we'd never know for sure when we got back to that first point. Or we could try to figure out how off course we are and try to plot a new course."

I should have bloody listened to him. I shouldn't have just assumed he was trying to take over. None of his actions or words pointed to that, just my prejudice. What was I going to say, I thought you were like my ex? Sorry I compared you to him? I reached up and smoothed my hair down and plaited it.

"Do you think either would work?"

"The second option is probably more promising."

He crouched and drew some lines in the sand. He showed me where we'd started, where we should have ended up and where we did end up. And the best way to get to the right spot.

"Do you think it will work?"

"All we can do is try."

CHAPTER EIGHT

Tyler

I STARED AT THE BED. It was nowhere near big enough for Makayla and I. I'd resigned myself to the fact that we'd be sharing a bed earlier, now I doubted a king-sized bed would be big enough. What had changed? Makayla had changed. We hadn't spoken since we left the desert and the air in the room was heavy with tension. There was more to her actions but she didn't divulge the details and I didn't ask.

"I'm going to get changed," she said. She grabbed her PJs out of her perfectly packed suitcase and headed to the bathroom.

My sleep shorts were near the top, but I had to dig further down into my not so neatly packed case to find my sleep shirt. I was neat at work but I was on holidays, I didn't need to be so neat now. Certainly not Makayla neat. Luckily I came prepared and actually packed a sleep shirt. Normally, I just slept in boxers but being away I thought I'd bring suitable bed clothes. I didn't rush. Makayla was likely to take her time just like she had earlier. I wasn't really pissed with her about hogging the bathroom, it was more the fact that she didn't seem to care that she left me hardly any time to get ready.

I put my sleepwear on, folded what I'd been wearing and threw it on top while I waited for Makayla. When she came out, she placed her perfectly folded clothes into her perfectly packed suitcase. I'd never met anyone who was so *perfect*.

By the time I got back from brushing my teeth Makayla was in bed. She was on her side, close to the edge with her back to the middle. That suited me just fine. I hopped into bed and mirrored her pose.

"Goodnight," I said as I switched off the light.

"Goodnight."

I lay there as still as a pinnacle and stared into the darkness. I wanted to roll onto my stomach. That's how I preferred to fall asleep. But I didn't want to disturb Makayla or touch her by accident. I didn't even want to breathe in her direction. I might get accused of stealing all the oxygen. OK. I was being stupid. There was more to Makayla than just bad manners. Something flipped the switch, but I had no idea what it was.

I lay staring into the darkness waiting for sleep to overcome me and wishing for it to hurry up. My body clock would wake me early, just like it would at home for a morning gym session. But no matter how much I willed it, sleep took forever to arrive.

I STOOD in the shower enjoying the hot water. I'd been in here a while and I imagined Makayla pacing the room. With twenty-five minutes left before we had to board the bus, I got out and dried myself at a leisurely pace. Was it childish? Hell yeah. Did I care? Nope. I grinned. Payback was a bitch. When my watch hit the twenty-minute mark, I picked up my things and strolled out of the bathroom.

"All yours," I said, giving Makayla a broad smile.

She marched into the bathroom, shutting the door firmly behind her. I packed my suitcase as I waited. I could have left the room without her, and although she deserved a little punishment, there was no reason to be downright rude. I put my case outside the door and waited on the bed.

Makayla had not spoken to me about last night. When we couldn't find our way and needed to be picked up, she had fallen silent. Every time I went to speak to someone she would cringe.

I switched my phone on and googled *Diary of a Wombat*. I couldn't help being curious about this *interesting* fact. The cover had me smiling before I could stop myself. A wombat lay on its side, so content in its sleep an earthquake probably wouldn't wake it, with a bunch of carrots nearby. I hit the buy button and started reading. As I turned the pages my smile grew. What a funny wombat.

The bathroom door opened and I clicked out of my screen. Without giving me a glance, Makayla shoved her things into her suitcase and zipped it closed. I jumped off the bed.

"Ready?"

"No thanks to you," she mumbled. Her voice may have been quiet but it held a distinct edge.

"Maybe you'll learn about sharing." I smiled on the inside. At least I gave her five more minutes than she gave me.

She grunted and walked out the door. What a beautiful morning—falling in love with a cheeky girl wombat and getting sweet revenge on the woman I shared a room with. We parked our cases near the trailer and headed to the bus. The cocky was on the door greeting guests, and Makayla in particular. He'd found his favourite target.

"We've got one. We've got one. Bed hair. Bed hair. Nooky nooky."

Makayla's long brown hair was indeed messy. She mustn't have had time to wash it. I hadn't thought of that when I'd left her so little time. I wouldn't do that again. The bird wolf whistled. Makayla glared at it and I followed suit.

Frank and Craig gave each other a nudge and smirk. My jaw clenched. There was no need for that behaviour. It was men like that that gave others a bad name.

I followed Makayla onto the bus, ignoring the two men. As soon as she reached her seat, she started to talk to her friends in hushed tones.

"How was your first night with a woman?" Harrison goaded.

I rolled my eyes. I had spent the night with women before. "I have never met anyone so painful. Yesterday she took forever in the bathroom and left me hardly any time to get ready. So, this morning I returned the favour."

Manny looked at me wide eyed. "You can't treat her like you would Clarissa."

Harrison nodded. "Yeah, she's not your sister."

"Clarissa, Makayla, what's the difference? Insolence is the same, regardless."

Manny shook his head. I shrugged. I did feel bad. Well, a little bit, but I wasn't going to tell them that.

"What happened last night?" Harrison asked, leaning across Manny so I didn't have to speak loudly. "We thought for sure your skills would win it."

I grunted. "I was sabotaged by Miss Insolence over there." I lifted my chin towards Makayla.

I didn't speak to them about it on the way back from the desert. Makayla and I hadn't been able to find our way out of the muddle we'd found ourselves in—we'd never found our next clue. On the bus ride back, I kept going over different scenarios in my head, trying to figure out what we could have done to fix it. It was impossible because there were too many variables.

"What do you mean?" Manny asked, looking at Makayla and her friends.

"She took charge. Wouldn't share the instructions with me. Wouldn't listen."

Harrison let out a low whistle.

"I don't even know what set her off." I shook my head. Women were impossible to figure out. "When we started heading in the wrong direction, I tried to tell her but she refused to admit she could have gotten it wrong."

"Really? This is the Makayla who barely spoke the first night we met?"

"Oh yeah. And then to top it off she accused me of mansplaining."

Harrison and Manny laughed. I'm glad they thought it was funny. I'd never been accused of trying to be superior in my life. I'd always thought I'd treated others equally, regardless of gender. I'm sure my colleagues didn't just humour me into thinking that. They always felt free to tell me when they disagreed, why would they hold back if I was being sexist?

And yet, this woman who had only just met me, had made up some preconceived ideas on who she thought I was. That was just bullshit. I glanced at her and her friends. They were all looking at me. Their eyes darted away.

"I've never met anyone so impossible in my life."

Manny and Harrison laughed again.

"What?"

"Have you met yourself?" Manny said.

"I never thought you'd meet someone as stubborn as you," Harrison added.

"I'm not stubborn. I'm determined. Regardless, I still respect the opinion of others," I pointed out.

They nodded. I'd built my reputation on that. I didn't become senior vice president by the time I was thirty by stepping on people's toes. I'd learnt from the best and built my team around me. I had a good relationship with my customers and team. But she'd shut me down before I'd even had a chance to speak.

Before we'd started the challenge, I'd thought about kissing her. I don't even know where the thought had come from. Maybe it was the quietness or the stars or the way she spoke about them exploding. Whatever it was, it didn't last long. Her actions made sure of that.

I reminded myself that I wasn't *interested* in Makayla. I didn't *want* to kiss her. Hell no. I shook my head. That wouldn't be smart, it would be like inviting all kinds of complicated into my life. The only complicated I needed was customers who tested our capabilities on delivering the near impossible.

Makayla snuck another look back at me. What on earth

were they talking about? I was pretty sure I hadn't done anything wrong in the whole scenario. OK, I could admit that hogging the bathroom this morning was wrong, but that one thing couldn't be what they were talking about all that time.

CHAPTER NINE

Makayla

"WAS HE MAD?" Nicki asked. We hadn't talked about the challenge when we got back on the bus last night. When they'd asked, I'd just shrugged. It was bad enough that I'd ruined the night. I didn't need to give a rendition of it as well. And when we got back to the motel, we all went to our separate rooms.

"No. Not even a hint of aggravation in his voice. He questioned me but he was more exasperated than anything else."

"M would have told everyone listening on the radio that it was your fault. All Tyler said was 'we,'" Nicki said. It appeared that none of us were to say Mitchell's name even if we were thinking about him. Ironic, really, that we all had the same thought. If we all thought of him at the same time, did that mean none of us had to do a task?

I nodded. I didn't give Tyler enough credit for that. He did not belittle me. He did not make me feel stupid. If it had been Mitchell, it would have been different and I probably would still be putting up with his petulance now. Once, we were late for a dinner with his colleagues because I couldn't figure out how to get into the carpark, and when I did, I parked in the wrong section, which meant we had to take one lift down and another one up. He didn't let it rest even when one of the partners said he'd done the same thing the first time he'd eaten at that restaurant. Every time we went for dinner after that, he insisted we leave home early in case I got lost again. Heaven forbid, he actually drive.

"Do you think that maybe you projected your feelings about what M would have been like in the hunt onto Tyler?" Rosanna asked, her voice soft.

"Maybe."

"Like M would have taken over from the beginning and would not have let you play an active role?"

I didn't need to ask myself if that would have happened because I knew it would. I had given ten years of my life to Mitchell. I'd held him on a pedestal. I couldn't admit to myself, let alone my friends, that the relationship was not what it was cracked up to be. Some days I still hoped there was a future for us. That my dream of us living in an upmarket suburb with two children where we had everything we needed was still possible. That had been Mitchell's dream too. Maybe we could make it reality. But did I really want to be with someone who made me feel insecure? Who didn't allow me to have my own voice?

"I think you need to apologise to Tyler," Rosanna said.

Nicki nodded. "I agree. It will complete your deed from yesterday."

"You only have six hours left, but I guess we can extend it until you're alone with him again."

They were right. I'd treated him badly. I'd said sorry but that sorry needed some explanation. It would be respectful and if I was him, I would appreciate it if someone afforded me that much effort. He deserved that much.

I glanced back at him and found him looking right at me. My stomach flipped.

WE STOOD on the paved circular area of the HMAS Sydney II Memorial and looked up at the dome set on columns. It was made of metal with some kind of pattern. I looked closer. Birds. The dome was hundreds of birds with outspread wings. I glanced around at our group, all waiting for our guide to speak. He gazed over the site before taking a deep breath and resting his gaze on us.

"On 19 November 1941, Australia suffered its worst naval loss. The HMAS *Sydney*, who was once the pride of the fleet, nicknamed the 'lucky ship' after surviving air strike after air strike in the Mediterranean, was sunk off the West Australian coast. Six hundred and forty-five men were on board. None survived." The Geraldton tour guide stood between us and the dome. "It had engaged with the German raider *Kormoran*. Both ships sunk."

Those words *none survived* echoed in my brain. Such a waste of life.

"This site is a memorial to those men."

He turned. We looked out to the ocean with him and goosebumps erupted on my skin. His attention came back to the dome.

"This is called the dome of souls. These birds represent

those souls that went down with the ship. All 645 of them. The seven pillars supporting the dome represent the seven states and territories of Australia. The floor below is made of cut stone from each of those states and territories."

I couldn't take my eyes off the birds. Each bird represented a man. A man whose life had been cut short. A man who never returned home to his family. My heart ached in a chest that felt so empty. I felt empty. Losing my future had left me feeling that way, but that didn't compare to losing your life. I still had hope.

We followed the guide to a semi-circular wall made of black stone. "The shape of this wall depicts the encircling arms welcoming home its lost ones. On this side of the wall are the names, ranks and home base of our 645 men."

THE REST IS SILENCE was engraved into the first panel. I took a deep breath trying to hold back my tears. Those men would be forever encompassed in the silence of the sea. Those left behind would have silence in their hearts. The air, our world, would no longer hear the men's voices. Just silence. Fathoms of silence.

"This tall structure over here is known as a stele." He was pointing to a tall upright column that reached metres in the air. "You can find steles around the world marking graves. This one is the likeness of the prow of the HMAS *Sydney II*."

Every element of this memorial had been thought out. Every part had a meaning. It showed thoughtfulness and respect—everything those heroes deserved. We walked over to some terraced stairs which led down to a circular pool. A single steel bird flew above it, the tip of its wing in the water.

"This is the Pool of Remembrance. It was designed to

show the descending to the depths to symbolise where the ship now lays."

Everyone stood quiet, solemn, staring into the water.

"The floor of the pool is a map and where that gull's wing tip is, is the place the Sydney rests."

Rests in silence.

"Now we will meet the Waiting Woman."

We followed him to the statue of a woman holding onto her hat, her dress flowing in the wind, looking out to sea. The sadness on her face brought fresh tears to my eyes. Who was she waiting for? Her husband? Her son? How many days did she wait, looking desperately out to sea for the ship to return? I couldn't imagine not knowing, having no finality, knowing that he was out there...somewhere. The emptiness would be everlasting. The others started to move away. I stayed, wanting to keep her company a little longer. She would be waiting, alone, forever and I felt some sort of connection with her. I knew what waiting felt like. I'd waited for Mitchell to return to me and our dreams. It wasn't the same. Not even close. But grief was grief. Hers was forever, mine didn't need to be.

Tyler was still there, standing in front of the statue, looking out to sea.

I took a deep breath in and closed my eyes. The breeze in my ears took away my sense of place. Heavy thunder echoed; shots fired from both ships hit their target. Unsteadiness took over as the ship rolled beneath me. Shouts from the sailors. I sucked a breath in and opened my eyes. The Waiting Woman still stood by my side and Tyler still stared out to sea.

I turned to see everyone else had disappeared.

"Tyler," I said, hesitant. "We need to go."

He faced me, his eyes shining. He regarded the woman, a sad smile on his face. He didn't try to hide his depth of feeling as he came to my side. We walked together in silence. I was drawn to him and the enormity of his emotions. The heat radiating off him warmed my arm. If I held his hand, would he understand that I felt it too—the sadness, the despair?

That was stupid. We didn't share anything profound. Anyone could have shared these feelings. I moved away until I could no longer feel his heat. Most people with a heart would have felt something in this place. How could you not feel for those souls lost at the bottom of the ocean and the loved ones they'd left behind? Mitchell would have felt it.

I shook my head. Comparing Tyler to Mitchell was ridiculous. One had held my heart for ten years and the other I'd only met days before. Sharing one moment with him was nothing compared to what I'd shared with Mitchell. And it's not even like we'd shared it. We were standing apart, lost in our own minds.

I needed to let Mitchell go and relinquish my dreams of living the perfect life with him. He was not what I needed anymore. What I needed was to be myself—not to be afraid to speak, to act, to make mistakes. I needed to forgive myself. One decision, one choice, could change your life but it didn't need to hold you prisoner.

I needed to choose myself.

CHAPTER TEN

Tyler

I LAY in bed beside Makayla. A little closer to the middle this time. Makayla's breathing beside me was irregular, telling me she wasn't asleep yet. We'd had a good afternoon in Geraldton visiting the museum and then having dinner with the group at the hotel restaurant. Makayla didn't share much about herself but I did learn that she was a counsellor. The way she listened to everyone and paid attention to what they said gave me the impression she was good at her job. That was a rare quality in people. They often only asked questions to be polite, but she seemed genuinely interested.

"Tyler?" Makayla's voice broke the silence.

"Yeah?"

"I'm sorry about yesterday."

"OK." I stayed still, waiting to hear what she had to say. Interested about what made her behave the way she did.

"I'm sorry about taking all that time in the shower. I was nervous about spending time alone with you."

"That's OK." That's not what I had expected her to say. I thought she was just being self-indulgent. I didn't consider that she was feeling as nervous as I was. The silence drew out. Was she going to say something else? "I'd be nervous about spending time with me, too. You wouldn't want to be corrupted by my hot body and cute smile."

She laughed. "Bloody Nicki."

My chest expanded. Thank goodness she'd taken that lightly.

"I'm sorry about how I acted during the navigation task." She took a breath as if steeling herself for what was coming next. "My ex, he liked to control everything. He would have taken over and I would have just been left following. I thought you might do the same, so I took over before you got the chance. I know it was wrong to think you were like him. You're not like him. I should have thought about it when you said that we should be working as a team. I should have realised then that you weren't trying to take over. And then when you tried to point out that we weren't going the right direction I should have respected that and listened to you."

She had said it all in a rush and I wasn't sure if she was finished. She wasn't.

"Thank you for not making me feel stupid and for not telling everyone it was my fault. And for not being angry with me."

"Apology accepted." I wanted her to feel better, so I added, "I think we're even on the shower front now."

She gave a small laugh.

Her ex sounded like a complete arse. Is that why she didn't talk much? Why sometimes she was self-conscious? The bed moved as she adjusted position. My fingers twitched.

How far would I have to reach out to touch her? What was I even thinking? I didn't want to touch Makayla. She was a whole world of trouble I wasn't prepared for. But the way her whole face lit up when she smiled or laughed lifted me in ways it shouldn't have. The way I felt connected to her at the memorial was unlike me.

Makayla shifted again. She'd barely moved last night. Maybe she usually tossed and turned but couldn't sleep last night because of our closeness. I know I had trouble sleeping.

"I don't feel well," she said into the darkness.

She shoved the covers aside and ran to the bathroom before I could even ask her what she meant.

The sound of her throwing up reached me. It continued for a couple of minutes. I waited for the toilet to flush and the tap to turn on. Nothing. I couldn't just leave her there suffering alone.

I went into the bathroom and found Makayla sprawled on the tiled floor. As I walked in, she hopped up and went for another round. I pulled the towels off the rack and folded one for her to kneel on and put the other down for her to lie on. Her hair was falling in her face. Clarissa hated it when vomit got in her hair. She said the smell lasted forever.

Hair tie. I needed a hair tie. I found Makayla's toiletry bag on the counter, and thankfully, her hair brush next to it. I was not particularly interested in looking in a lady's toiletry bag. Who knows what I would find? Hair ties were twisted around the handle of the hair brush. I grabbed one off.

Makayla half kneeled, half sat on the ground, her arms crossed over the toilet seat and her head resting in her arms.

"I'm just going to tie your hair back," I said as I approached her.

She gave me a small nod. I pulled her hair back, being careful not to be rough and put it in a ponytail. I rested my hand on the back of her neck—warm and clammy.

"Lay down on the towel if you need to rest."

Again, a small nod. A few moments passed before she let go of the toilet and lay down.

"Thank you," she said, her voice barely above a whisper.

How many times had I looked after Clarissa like this? Too many to count. I hadn't known how to tie a ponytail at first but I'd soon learnt.

I grabbed a face washer and wet it down before pressing it against Makayla's neck. I sat on the floor next to her until I was convinced she wasn't going to be sick again.

"Makayla, come back to bed. It will be more comfortable there."

She nodded but didn't make a move.

"Come on. I'll take the waste bin with us in case you feel sick again."

She nodded and sat up. I crouched and put my arms under hers to help her up. "Do you want to rinse your mouth out first?"

She nodded and I led her to the sink. I got her a glass of water, so she could rinse, and then followed her back to bed. Putting the bin down, I sat beside her on the edge and then rubbed her back like I used to do with Clarissa. She always said it helped her, comforted her.

When I was sure Makayla was asleep, I went back to my side.

But sleep wouldn't come. Instead, images of Clarissa flung themselves around my head. Her body changing over time as the sickness took over. Where she was once soft, bones had started to stick out. How she would cry because we didn't know what was wrong with her. The ambulance taking her away to a place I couldn't visit, where she could find some mental and emotional stability. Me waiting on the doorstep, day after day, week after week, for her to come home.

Makayla shifted beside me. I wanted to reach my hand out, to touch her, to reassure myself she wasn't going anywhere.

But she wasn't Clarissa. And it didn't really matter if she left.

I slept on and off. Always listening and alert as dreams and pictures raced around my mind. Light entered around the curtains as night transformed into day. The music from my alarm reminded me that time doesn't wait for anyone. Tiredness or sickness made no difference to the second hand. I switched off the alarm as Makayla rolled onto her back and stared at the roof. How creepy was it that I just laid there watching her?

CHAPTER ELEVEN

Makayla

"How are you feeling?" Tyler asked. He was awake early again, just like the other morning. I was not an early riser, preferring to start my day slowly, by hitting the snooze button a few times.

"Much better. Must have been something I ate. I'm never sick."

Tyler nodded. I swear that man was a saint. No one had ever looked after me like he had last night.

He rolled onto his back and his shoulder touched mine. I took a deep, satisfied breath and laid my arm next to his so I could feel his steadiness. My skin welcomed his, almost like it had been waiting for it. Being here, with him, was both natural and unnatural. If he had wrapped me in his arms right then I would have yielded to him and never wanted to leave.

What the hell?

I sat up and swung my legs out of bed. Lack of sleep and

his caring ways had my brain thinking all kinds of weird things.

"I'm going to shower." I stood up and walked to the bathroom. Clothes. I needed clothes. I also needed to thank him... with a kiss. What? No. Why was I even thinking about kissing him? Those lips that were always ready to tease and give me that lopsided smile did not need my lips on them. I did not need my lips on them or anywhere on his body. No lips.

I shook my head and walked to my case, grabbing a dress out. Frank had said we would be doing a few hours of driving so I figured a dress would be more comfortable.

Tyler shifted on the bed. I snuck a peak at him to find he was on the phone typing. Was he texting someone? I shook my head. What did it matter if he was? It was none of my business.

"I won't be long," I said as I stood up.

"OK." He looked up and smiled. "I'll just reply to some emails while I wait."

Was I that boring that he decided to work? I traipsed to the bathroom and grabbed the towels off the floor. I hung one up for Tyler and took the other with me to hang outside the shower. The hot water made me feel better.

Why had it bothered me that Tyler was working? Mitchell is why it bothered me. He was always more interested in work than in me. I'd told myself he was working so hard to build our future. He said real estate didn't stop for a relationship and I'd accepted that. But Tyler wasn't ignoring me. He hadn't picked up the phone until he thought I was going to shower. And really, we were nothing more than roommates—two people sharing a bed sounded too intimate—so it didn't matter if he was working while I showered.

It would be better if he were in the shower with me.

My breath caught. I needed to stop this shit. Fantasising about someone who was your opposite was stupid. Like how he was messy – his suitcase looked like a jumbled mess. Just the thought of it had me cringing. And how he was chipper in the morning where I preferred to be like a teenager, warming up to the day. In my eyes it was acceptable enough to act human in the morning, I didn't need to act happy as well. And then there was his clothing and sunglasses, all upmarket compared to my Kmart wardrobe. Opposites in so many ways. His compassion, as attractive as it was, was irrelevant.

I could have stayed under the water all day but that would be rude. I'd done it to Tyler on the first night and he had paid me back good and proper. I reached for the towel. Thank goodness it didn't smell like vomit. I dried myself and got dressed before giving my teeth a quick brush. I couldn't taste vomit anymore, thanks to Tyler suggesting rinsing, but the mint freshness was better.

TYLER and I walked to breakfast together. As we crossed the carpark, I lifted my face up to the sun, enjoying how it heated my cheeks.

"Thank you for looking after me last night."

"You're welcome."

What? No teasing? And he didn't big-note himself by pointing out how he cared for a sick person.

Frank was at the door to greet us. He glanced between us and gave us a sleazy smile.

"Looks like you two didn't get much sleep." He nudged

Tyler and gave him a wink.

"Makayla was sick." Tyler's words had a hard edge that even an idiot couldn't miss.

"Oh, right. I hope you're feeling better now," he said, watching me.

"Yes, thank you." I was lucky to have Tyler, I added to myself.

We headed to the table where our friends were waiting.

"You look like shit," Rosanna said.

"You're so kind. I didn't sleep well. Something I ate didn't agree with me."

"Bummer. How are you feeling now?"

"Better. Hungry."

I didn't need to say another word. Everyone hopped up and we headed to the buffet.

"Are you alright, Ty?" Harrison asked from behind.

"Yeah, long night. I couldn't sleep once we got back to bed."

"I bet. It must have reminded you of Clarissa."

There was that name again. Tyler didn't answer. I rounded the buffet so I could look at Tyler and not make it obvious. Manny gave his shoulder a squeeze.

"Did Tyler look after you?" Nicki whispered.

I walked faster to get away from the others. The hot food side of the buffet called out to me, but that wasn't the only reason I walked faster. I wouldn't have a chance to speak to Nicki and Rosanna alone for a few hours. And there were way too many confusing thoughts going through my head that I needed to share.

"Yeah. He came into the bathroom and sat with me for over an hour making sure I was OK."

"Wow." Rosanna nodded appreciatively.

"Even when we got back to bed, he sat with me and rubbed my back."

"Is that man even real?" Nicki said, glancing at Tyler as we rounded the buffet. "He's got a body like a dream—"

"How do you know?" I asked. She raised her eyebrows at me and grabbed two slices of bread and put them in the toaster. I hoped it would take a long time to cook so we had more time to talk.

Nicki glanced over at the guys grabbing eggs and bacon. The thought of eggs was not appealing, but I'd loaded up on the bacon. "Girl, blind Freddy couldn't miss that. Lucky he didn't keep his shirt up for longer that first night, I might have actually drooled."

Rosanna nodded. "I'm glad he wears a t-shirt so I can see his muscles flex when he picks something up."

"Yum."

"OMG. You two are bad." I turned and put more bread in the toaster so they couldn't see my smile. His muscles were good, not huge like a body builder's, but nicely defined. Yeah, his muscles were good.

"He doesn't have abs like a magazine model," Rosanna said.

A hand went to my hip. "You can't go around objectifying men. And you can't comment on their lack of abs, that's like body shaming. You know that's a problem in society for men and women."

Nicki ignored me. "Who needs abs when you look that good? Flat. Toned. Mmm."

"How long did you look for?"

I was aware the guys were getting closer.

Rosanna giggled. "The whole time."

"You can't say you haven't noticed," Nicki said.

I wasn't saying any such thing. But I also wasn't admitting that I had. Or that he was drool worthy.

The three men walked up to us. Rosanna grabbed the toast we had just cooked from the tray and handed it over to them.

"Thanks," Tyler said, taking two pieces.

"Don't mention it. It's the least we could do after you looked after Mak."

The other two took the remaining pieces.

"Well, skedaddle along now. We haven't finished talking about you yet." Rosanna flicked her hands at them.

My face burned. I spun around and put more bread in the toaster.

Manny laughed before turning away. "Must be talking about you, Ty."

"What the hell, Rosanna?" I angry whispered.

"We didn't need them standing there all day. There is a time limit for this breakfast you know."

I shook my head.

"So, are you going to give him a proper thank you later?" she asked.

What was she suggesting?

"Like a kiss?" Nicki said.

"No."

"But you've thought about it, haven't you?" Nicki pressed.

"No."

"You so have. You denied it too quickly."

"I have not." I willed my toast to hurry up, not thinking about kissing Tyler. Or his lips. Or his body. Or *him*.

CHAPTER TWELVE

Tyler

"Ok. We're going to leave the bus and trailer here. We'll grab the overnight bags you packed this morning and head to the four-wheel drives." We were in a carpark at the back of a servo. Frank pointed out the windows to the six four-wheel drives waiting for us. "Myself and Chris as well as our local guides will be doing the driving."

We filed off the bus and headed to the trailer. I grabbed my bag and stood next to Makayla. Frank moved among us splitting us up into groups of four. He stopped in front of us. "I need four of you in one car and two in another."

I glanced around our group.

"It's really up to you and Makayla who you want to go with," Manny said.

Everyone else nodded. Since when had we been chosen as the token couple? Makayla said nothing. Red rose on her cheeks just as it had at breakfast. She couldn't have been more obvious if she tried. I kept my smile to myself.

"I think you should come with us," Rosanna said.

"For sure." Nicki smiled at Rosanna in a way that made me nervous.

"OK then." Frank pointed. "Hop into the car over there."

Harrison and Manny both smirked.

"Good luck," Manny said.

I didn't find him amusing in the least. The last time I'd spent a significant amount of time with three females was with Clarissa and her friends and they had peppered me with questions that would make any male want to run for their life. *Why is it OK for men to have had many sexual partners but not women? Boobs or arse, what's your preference? Why? How old were you when you lost your virginity? Why are you single?* What I needed to do was lead this conversation.

Makayla slid into the middle seat and I hopped in beside her. She fumbled with her seatbelt, grabbing my arse at one point. I shuffled my butt out of the way as she mumbled an apology. I didn't need to look at her to know she was blushing again. Then it was my turn to buckle. I made a conscious effort not to fondle her.

"So, Nicki, what made you decide to be a scientist?" I asked as we started driving.

"The three of us took STEM classes at high school and even entered competitions. We did the National Science Challenge and Mathletics right up to year 12. I loved it."

"Nicki was the science queen, Mak was an ace at maths, and I was just along for the ride," Rosanna said from the other side of Makayla.

"Yeah, you think being Asian she would lead in all things academic." Nicki laughed. "But the only reason she came along was because she didn't want to miss out."

"To be fair, she did contribute to our success," Makayla said.

"True, it just wasn't her passion like it was ours."

"Why didn't you pursue maths?" I asked Makayla.

She looked at her hands and took a deep breath. I'd obviously asked the wrong question.

Nicki turned around and gave Makayla a smile. "Mak was set for a scholarship. She had reached the top five in Australia. Then at a Mathletics comp she questioned a judge's qualifications when he awarded a point incorrectly."

Rosanna took over. "It was a tight competition, only a couple of points in it. Makayla was right, he'd awarded a point incorrectly. But the way she questioned him, right there in front of everyone. You could hear the gasps around the room. He was on the scholarship committee."

My heart sank.

"That was it. The scholarship was gone," Nicki said.

If I could have disappeared, I would have. That one moment sounded like a crushing moment in her life. I should have just let them lead the conversation. Stupid.

Makayla stiffened her shoulders, faced me and gave me a smile. "It led me to a more satisfying career. What I do now makes a difference to students' lives." Her voice was strong, resolute even though her shoulders sagged just a little. She may have had regrets that haunted her but she hadn't let them stop her from moving forwards.

Makayla took a deep breath and lifted her head. "When a study was done years ago, 5,000 students were asked to draw a scientist. Do you know how many drew that scientist as a female?"

I shook my head.

"Twenty-eight. Twenty-eight out of 5,000. That was back in the seventies. Studies done in later years showed that 73% of children drew the scientist as male, and that percentage rose as students got older."

That was terrible. I'd never thought of females being underrepresented in certain careers. And I certainly didn't know it could be traced back to childhood beliefs. The truth was I was just ignorant to it.

"At aged six, 70% of females drew female scientists. By age ten it was less than 50% and by high school only 20% of females drew scientists as female."

She sounded like a true mathematician, still, with her use of statistics. I shook my head at the numbers. They were staggering. Wrong. And my complacency and ignorance, just like others in society, was a contributing factor. "I didn't realise."

"Not many do. That's why what I do is important. I want to change those beliefs one student at a time. If they show an interest in science, I encourage it. If they decide it might be a career they want to look into, I guide them."

Nicki spoke from the front seat. "She invites me to do a talk every year. It's great. I love interacting with the students. Mak selects twenty students and we spend all day talking science and doing experiments."

How many other career paths did this lack of inclusivity cross? I thought of my own office. There weren't many females there. And there wasn't one in an executive position.

"Do you know the number of females in investment banking?" Makayla asked as if reading my mind.

"No."

"Ten percent."

What could I say to that? It was appalling. And worse

was to think whether I had contributed to that in some way. How could I make a difference? Maybe talk to other banks about increasing the number of females. But females rarely applied for the jobs. Did I need to go back further like Mak did?

The driver stopped the car on the side of the road and opened the door. "We're heading off the bitumen now so I need to let down the tyres."

Rosanna looked around Mak to me and asked, "Why is he letting air out of the tyres?"

"It makes the ride more cushiony over rough tracks."

"How?"

"It means the tyres can mould to the bumps in the tracks. Then when we hit sand, the lower pressure means there is more surface area contacting the ground."

"How does that help?"

"It means the tyres are less likely to sink into the sand and we won't get bogged."

She nodded and sat back in her seat. Lucky my dad took us out camping when I was younger or else I probably wouldn't have known that answer. Did she ask me just because I'm a male? Maybe not. Maybe she knew Mak and Nicki didn't know.

As we set off again, I studied the landscape. Sand and low shrubs spread to the horizon on both sides of the track. The further we drove the worse the corrugations got. We bounced around in the back. Mak bumped against me, her boobs bouncing up and down. I tried not to notice but she was in a dress and was right next to me. The only way I couldn't see was by staring out the window. If I were to be honest, I'd rather stare at her boobs.

Rosanna was giggling. "It's like your boobs are doing a jig, Mak."

Nicki turned to have a look. I couldn't help doing the same. The three of them looked at me and raised their eyebrows.

"What? You were the ones who pointed them out."

Nicki smirked and faced the front. Rosanna whispered something to Mak that made her pull away from me. When she bumped into me, she tried to move away but the dips in the road pushed her back. We weren't going fast and every bump we hit felt like it was going to shake my bones loose. The distance may have been short but it seemed like forever to get there. The sandy hills were just as bumpy. Even the beach was bumpy.

"We're camping at Shelter Bay. It's a great spot, sheltering us from the southerlies. We'll set up camp, have some lunch and head out for a little look see," the driver said.

As I gazed out the window, the white beach and crystal-clear water made the rattling and bumps fade into insignificance. Not Makayla's breasts though.

CHAPTER THIRTEEN

Makayla

"OK. If you can help me get the tents off the roof, then grab a tent, and we'll head to the beach," our driver said.

I slid out after Tyler and followed him around the back. The driver hooked a step up over the wheel and hopped up to grab three tents off. Tyler helped him get them all down, then I took hold of a handle and Tyler grabbed the other one. We followed the driver.

"I can't believe we're camping on the beach," I said.

"I know. Not many people can say they've camped on a beach."

"Have you?"

"Yeah. I should really get back into camping. I haven't been for years."

The driver stopped in a sandy clearing. "Right. We're going to set your group's camp up here. I'll show you how to put up the tent and then I'll start unloading the supplies from the car. The other groups will be scattered along the beach."

He dragged the tent in the bag across the ground to level out the sand. Then he pulled the tent out of the bag and rolled it out. I stood close to Tyler watching the driver. He stepped into the empty space made by the open door of the tent that still lay on the ground, grabbed hold of the roof bar and pulled it forwards. Within seconds the tent was standing.

"Wow," I said. "I never thought putting up a tent would be so easy."

"OK. Now I just need to peg it down, pull out the awning and I'm done."

"Ready?" Tyler asked me.

"Yep. I'll do it."

He nodded and let me do it on my own. He didn't offer advice. Didn't try to take over. He didn't say the sand wasn't flat enough or the tent was in the wrong spot. Nothing.

"Let's go help bring the other supplies over," he said when I'd finished.

He didn't act like my place was at the campsite and his was to do the manly work. Our bags were the first to come out. I did my best to ignore how he haphazardly placed his in the tent. But I couldn't. When he walked out, I straightened it up next to mine. His classy leather duffle bag next to my striped cotton weekender bag; two ends of the spectrum. Like Tyler and I. He was all style...and I wasn't.

We continued unloading the car. He didn't automatically hand me the light things. He just handed me whatever he pulled out.

When he got to the esky, I tried to lift it but it was too heavy. When I shook my head, he didn't say anything, just went and grabbed something else for me to carry. We continued our quiet work until the car was unpacked and the campsite set up and then headed to the main camp for lunch. The talk was all about the Point which we were soon going to see

---

"THESE ARE THE ZUYTDORP CLIFFS," our guide announced as we hopped out of the car. "They're named after a Dutch ship wrecked there in 1712."

We followed him out to get a closer view. Rugged red limestone cliffs stretched as far as the eye could see. The sound of the waves crashing against the cliffs grew louder the closer we got to the edge. The base of the cliffs cut ragged through the blue sea. The cliff faces weren't smooth; they reminded me of calloused palms like those of the woodwork teacher at school. Rough. Timeworn.

I stepped closer to the edge. The wind in my ears and the thunder of the waves blocked out the voices of those around me. I turned to see where Tyler was. He stood a few feet behind me. I beckoned him forwards but he shook his head.

The colour of the cliffs changed as if each layer told its own story. At the base it was dark, water from the pounding waves staining it. The stained rock rose much higher than I thought it would. The seas must have been powerful to reach those heights. If the fall from the cliffs didn't kill you, the battering from the ocean would.

I closed my eyes. Emptiness. Air rushed past my ears, past my body. I felt light, as if the wind could pick me up. My heart pounded. I shook my head and my eyes sprung open. Logically, I knew I was still metres away from the edge, that the wind could not take me away. But the light-headedness didn't leave until I spun and walked away. I followed the group back to the car, catching snippets of Nicki and Tyler's conversation. I quickened my pace so I could hear more.

"It didn't really bother me when I was younger. I would climb trees with the best of them," Tyler said.

"What changed?"

"I'm not sure. All of a sudden heights just made me nervous."

"All heights?"

"Yeah. I'm not so bad in my office now, but I prefer not to get close to the window."

"What floor are you on?"

"Twenty second."

"Well, at least you didn't say third." Nicki laughed and elbowed Tyler in the arm. That was one way to make someone more relaxed about their fear. But I don't think Tyler needed help in that respect. He owned it without embarrassment.

We drove along the bumpy road until we reached Steep Point. We hopped out of our four-wheel drive and waited for Manny and Harrison to arrive.

"I've never been to any of the most extreme points in Australia," Rosanna said as we headed across the rocky ground to the sign saying we were at mainland Australia's most westerly point. The ocean stretched to the horizon, blue against blue. The ocean's blue was so deep and rich against the sky so pale it could almost be considered wishy-washy. Dirk Hartog Island, in the distance, was the only thing to break the continuity.

"I'll take a photo of you guys," Nicki said, over the wind. Her hair was blowing every which way.

Manny handed over his phone. Nicki took a few photos and then handed hers over to get a photo of us. I plaited my hair down my back to keep it under control.

"Here, let me take a photo of the group," our guide said. Nicki passed her phone over and we all stood around the sign. "And one of the happy couple," he said.

Everyone walked away leaving Tyler and me standing there.

"We're not a—"

"Stand closer together," the guide instructed, moving his hands closer together in case we couldn't hear over the wind.

I glanced at Tyler who just shrugged. I took a deep breath and stood closer to him. It was easier than trying to explain. Tyler put his arm around my shoulders. I put mine around his waist, just like I would any friend. *Friend*, I reminded myself as my body was drawn into his warmth.

———

"SO, what's happening with you and Tyler?" Rosanna asked as we walked along the beach.

"Nothing is happening between me and Tyler." Why had she asked? My hair was tamer now we were out of the wind and I released it from its plait.

"Really?" asked Nicki. "You didn't make a fuss about sharing a tent with him."

"You're basing your idea that something is going on between us because I'm sharing a tent with him?"

"You could have shared with us," Rosanna said.

"I've shared a room with him. Sharing a tent with him isn't much different."

"But today you had a choice," Nicki said.

"Yeah, you could have slept in our tent. There's room enough."

I clenched my fist. "There is nothing going on between Tyler and me."

"But there should be," Rosanna said with too much glee in her voice.

"For goodness' sake, I've known him for a few days."

"So?" Nicki asked.

"So, a few days isn't long enough to have something going on with someone."

"Some people get married a few hours after meeting." Nicki's voice was so matter of fact I wanted to slap her.

"Makayla, you had ten years with Mitchell. Ten wasted years," Rosanna said.

My jaw clenched. Why were they allowed to bring up his name if I wasn't?

"Mitchell and Tyler are two different people," Nicki said, her voice soothing compared to Rosanna's. "When you got lost in the desert did Tyler make a scene?"

"No."

It didn't mean anything. Just because he was polite did not mean I should have something going on with him. We'd been through this already. I don't know why it was so important they needed to bring it up again.

"Did he belittle you? Let everyone know it was your fault?"

"No." Why did I feel compelled to answer when they already knew?

"Did he get angry?"

I don't think angry was in Tyler's range of emotions. The

only time I'd seen him use any type of serious tone was when I questioned him about his dad and their camping trips, and when he told Frank I was sick. It was just the way he was, it had nothing to do with him being interested in me or that we should have something going on. More like the opposite. "He was just being nice because he doesn't know me."

"Right. And when he looked after you when you were sick, was he just being nice then?" Nicki pressed.

"Yes."

"Really? Your supposed fiancé would have just left you there to suffer alone," Rosanna said.

"Is this a good cop bad cop thing?" I asked. I walked along the water's edge; the gentle waves lapped at my feet. It was late afternoon and the water was warmer than I expected.

"Don't change the subject," Rosanna said, shoving me.

"What is with you two? There are plenty of nice guys out there. Why are you fixated on Tyler?"

"Tyler is here. They are not."

"I'm not interested in Tyler."

The pair of them looked at each other.

"Why don't one of you go for him if he's so fantastic?"

"Because he doesn't look at us like he does you."

They were imagining things.

"Stop wasting your time thinking about Mitchell," Rosanna said. "He's not worth it."

"Why didn't you mention this last year? Or five years ago? Or ten?"

"I'm pretty sure we did, but losing that scholarship ...well, you latched onto someone you thought gave you stability," Nicki said.

Rosanna took my hand. "But in the end your dreams were

your own. The plan you had, Mitchell said he shared it, but he didn't."

She was right.

"Now, back to Tyler," Nicki said.

I rolled my eyes. "I'm not interested in Tyler."

"Come on, not even a little bit?"

Wanting to be in his embrace did not mean I was interested in him. Thinking about kissing him did not mean I was interested in him. Willingly sharing a tent with him did not mean I was interested in him.

"No." I whirled around and headed back in the direction of our campsite.

"Huh. You hesitated too long," Rosanna said. She laughed as she caught up to me and pushed me again.

"We're not saying you need to marry the guy. Just enjoy your time with him," Nicki encouraged.

"Yeah. He has much more going for him than Mitchell."

"He wasn't afraid to admit his fear about heights, yes, I know you were listening. And he showed emotion at the memorial," Nicki said.

"I doubt Mitchell exposed himself like that once in ten years," Rosanna said.

"I bet Mak wants Tyler to expose himself." Nicki bumped into Rosanna who bumped into me.

"Hell, I want Tyler to expose himself." Rosanna smacked her lips together.

"For goodness' sake, you can have him then."

"Wrong answer." Rosanna pushed me. We both lost our footing. I tried to regain my balance, my arms flailing, reaching out for her. She was out of reach. She landed on her hands and knees in the shallows. My heart raced as I fell backwards, landing in the deeper water. I sat up, soaked from head to foot. Nicki helped Rosanna up and they laughed from the safety of the shoreline.

"Sorry. Gotta run. Maybe Tyler can help you get out of your wet clothes." Rosanna looped her arm through Nicki's and then walked away.

"Mmmm, imagine those strong hands..."

CHAPTER FOURTEEN

Tyler

I LOOKED up as Makayla came traipsing through the camp-site, her clothing wet. "What on earth?"

I got up and followed her into the tent.

"Are you OK?"

"Fine."

"Do you need some help?"

"I said I'm fine."

I took a step back, holding up my hands.

She turned on me as fast as a competitor in a takeover negotiation. "Why do you always have to be so nice?"

Being nice was a bad thing? I tilted my head. "You don't want me to be nice?"

"No."

I'd never heard of someone not wanting people to be nice. "What would you rather me be?"

"Not nice. Unlikeable."

My body felt light. "You like me?"

"No. I don't like you."

"But you said I was likable."

She stamped her foot and stared at me, her jaw set. "It doesn't mean I like you."

"So, I'm likable, but you don't like me?" I tried to hold my smile in.

She took two quick steps and was right up in my body space. "I don't like you. I'm not interested in you."

Her arms wrapped around my neck and her mouth crashed with mine. As quick as the kiss started, it finished.

Her wide eyes stared at me. She smoothed her top down which just made it cling to her body more. "Right. OK. Yep."

I opened my mouth but before I could say a word she whipped around and escaped from the tent. What had just happened? I stared after her as she walked to the edge of the campsite and paused. What an idiot. I should have kissed her back.

She spun around and marched back to the tent. When she stepped inside, she smoothed her top down again. The wetness exposed the top of her breasts. I'd be jerking off to that sight for a very long time.

"Sorry about that." She looked up at me and gave me a small smile.

"I'm not."

Slight movement caught my attention, she was flexing her fingers.

I pulled her towards me. As my lips met hers, she sighed. My dick went hard as her lips opened to mine. Her warm mouth invited me in as if it was a haven and I was lost at sea. She pressed against my body and I held her there savouring every morsel of her sweet taste.

Her hands pushed against my chest. Our bodies separated and then our lips. I breathed heavy as I stared down at her.

"I like it when you express yourself," I said, smiling.

She took a step back. My stomach dropped. Had I said the wrong thing?

"I need to get changed."

"Yes. OK." *I could help you with that* sat on the tip of my tongue. I walked out of the tent and joined our friends who were sitting around talking. They'd strategically left two empty seats next to each other.

"What happened to Makayla?" I asked.

"What happened to Makayla?" Rosanna repeated, loud enough for Makayla to hear in the tent. "We just had a bit of a disagreement about men."

I shut up then. There was no way I was getting involved in girl talk about men. I'd done that with Clarissa and her friends once and had regretted it for weeks. They'd twisted everything I said around onto me. You'd think they would have been grateful for some male insight. Wrong.

Manny shifted in his seat and rested his elbows on his knees. The smart arse wasn't going to let this go. "What sort of disagreement?"

Makayla came back out of the tent, her face serious. "That's none of your business."

"But if it's about our good friend Ty, it is our business," Manny said, leaning back and giving her a grin.

She stood there and stared him down. Then she went over to him, leant down and whispered something in his ear. His eyes widened and his mouth dropped open. She smiled like a banker who'd just won on the equity market. What had she said?

"This place is glorious," Rosanna said, looking out over the calm water, deftly changing the subject.

"I couldn't agree more," Harrison said. "Who would have thought we would be camping right on the beach?"

Manny looked over at me. "Remember that time we went camping at Johanna Beach?"

I nodded.

"It started out like this and then the wind picked up." Manny stood up, swaying. "Fair dinkum, the tent was moving like this." He leant so far over he was lucky to stay on his feet. "The four of us, Harrison, Tyler, Clarissa and I were huddled together in the middle."

Harrison shivered. "It was so cold and then the rain came."

"And it came." Manny sat in his chair.

It was bad. Even the memory had me tensing. "The tent we thought was waterproof was anything but."

Harrison nodded. "Poor Clarissa. I could hear her chanting to herself 'don't be sick, don't be sick'."

"And I was thinking 'let us live, let us live,'" I said.

"And, in between those chants she declared she'd never come camping with us again." Manny laughed.

"But she did," Harrison said. "She was such a trooper."

If nothing else, Clarissa was a trooper.

"WHO'S CLARISSA?" Makayla asked as we settled into our sleeping bags.

I couldn't describe everything Clarissa was, not in only a

few sentences. I took a deep breath and stared into the darkness. "Clarissa is my twin sister."

A barely audible sigh escaped from Makayla. Some shuffling and fumbling. "Is she sick?" Her voice was quiet, almost as if she was afraid to ask.

"She was sick. She's better now." The blackness of the tent squeezed me. Squeezed my lungs. The sadness and helplessness came crashing back. The sleeping bag constricted my movements. I yanked my arms out.

"Ty, it's OK. You don't need to talk about it."

"She had Cyclic Vomiting Syndrome." I paused. That wasn't quite correct. "I guess she still has it. It's just controlled now."

"What's Cyclic Vomiting Syndrome?"

"Imagine how you were sick the other night and multiply that by a hundred. It can last for hours or days."

And by days I meant days. When there was nothing left to vomit, she would just dry heave.

"Then there could be a few days, sometimes weeks, of normalcy before it started again." Shivers ran through me. I held my arms closer to me for comfort.

"There was misdiagnosis after misdiagnosis. She lost weight. She didn't want to go out. Everyone in the family was stressed. My parents argued. Clarissa and I would lock ourselves away and play games or read. Harrison and Manny would come over and keep us company."

My best friends were amazing. They'd never complained about not going out and meeting girls. They'd never made Clarissa feel bad for being sick. They just accepted it was part of her.

"When we were sixteen, she had a really bad bout. An

ambulance came and took her away. They wouldn't let me go with her. All I could do was watch it drive away with my sister inside. I didn't know if she would come back."

Tears welled in my eyes. It's hard to describe to people how close we are. We were born premature and spent months in the hospital together. The doctors found early on that if they tried to separate us, one or the other would deteriorate. When I'd grown strong enough to go home, they wouldn't allow it, knowing how detrimental it would be to Clarissa. Even as babies we had our own secret language.

That day, when they took her away, I'd stood there, watching the ambulance as it disappeared around the corner. My mum came over and put her hand on my shoulder. I jerked away from her. She was the one who'd called the ambulance. She was the one who said I couldn't go with Clarissa. Who would comfort her? Who would comfort me? I'd sunk to the ground, hugging my knees, crying.

"They took her to a psychiatric hospital. My world had been torn away." My voice broke. The way my mother looked at me that day made me feel like it was my fault. She didn't need to say the words because I felt them in my heart. Why Clarissa and not me? What if she died and I lived? If I asked when I could go to see her, she would say 'just leave her alone' or 'she doesn't need you there, Tyler'. My sister, my twin, didn't need me. I needed her. Maybe it *was* my fault. Maybe I was sucking the life out of her, making her sick. My dad would yell at her for saying such things, saying none of this was my fault. That maybe she should look at little closer to home. It was bad with Clarissa there; it was bad with her away. The torment never seemed to leave me.

"When I was short with you in the desert about my dad

taking us out to camp and do scavenger hunts, it was because you reminded me of my mother. She would criticise my dad about the camping trips. She thought they were a bad idea. But those times were the only times we felt like we weren't surrounded by Clarissa's illness." Maybe my mum resented that. I don't know. I think she was just unhappy. When Clarissa returned home it didn't take my mother long to leave. Maybe she had always wanted to leave but couldn't while Clarissa was sick. Maybe that's why she treated me the way she did.

Makayla moved beside me. Her warm hand took mine. All the excuses I made about not having a partner were just excuses. I could have made time. A relationship would not have affected my career. I'd always said being an investment banker was a lifestyle. It was a lie. Investment banking in Australia is nothing like in the United States. I wasn't expected to work 100 hours a week just to establish myself. No, I just didn't want to lose someone. I didn't want my heart broken so I didn't open it. I'd had relationships, short ones. As soon as they got serious, I backed away like a deal had gone sour.

"But she got better," Makayla said, bringing me out of my sinking thoughts.

"She had a wonderful doctor. He went through all of her case history. He saw everything that had been ruled out and did research in journals and called doctors overseas. He did test after test."

It had taken months. She had been locked in that place for months. But she didn't refer to it like that, not then or now. She said it was scary sometimes as some of the kids would act out or get violent. She wasn't with them but she could hear them. She called it her healing place.

"She was so positive, Makayla. Always. Even when she was in the hospital. She wrote me letters telling me all about the doctors and nurses and how they were all sure she would get better."

Those letters had given me hope. Clarissa must have known that and I loved her for it.

"As soon as she was diagnosed, they worked on discovering the triggers and trying different treatments. They found her triggers were a mixture of things—her period, stress and exhaustion. They dealt with those individually. It took a couple of months but they got it right."

And then she'd come home.

CHAPTER FIFTEEN

Makayla

I GAVE Ty's hand a squeeze. The way he spoke so openly and how his voice displayed his emotions surprised me. When I'd first met him, I'd thought his teasing and joking were immature, but there was much more to him than that. He's been through more than most people had. Maybe the humour was a shield.

He shifted beside me. Closer. His warmth caressed me.

"You know that camping story Manny and Harrison were talking about?"

I nodded. The silence stretched. Idiot, he couldn't see me nod. "The one with the wild wind?"

"Yeah." He laughed. "Manny and Clarissa told me they were an item that night. That one revelation tilted my axis."

What did he mean? He didn't seem to have a problem with Manny. Didn't he like that his best friend was dating his sister?

"Just knowing she had someone who loved her, all of her,

made me as happy as a pig in shit. I always knew she'd be OK on her own. She's tough. Resilient. But having love, true love is like...I don't know, being absolute."

Absolute. I'd never felt that before.

What had Ty said earlier? He liked it when I expressed myself. It had been a long time since I'd been able to do that. For ten years I'd curbed my personality, my thoughts and my feelings. I'd always fitted into what Mitchell needed, what he wanted. Tyler made me feel different. I felt free with him. Like I could do and say what I wanted and he would not admonish me.

Absolute. I wanted to feel absolute.

"Why didn't Clarissa come on the trip?"

"They are trialling different medications. She and Manny want to try for a baby, to do that she needs to come off the pill."

I smiled. That sort of bravery and love was sure to win out.

Ty shuffled closer and put his arm around me. My stomach flipped. I cradled myself in him.

"Thank you for listening," he said, his breath brushing my hair.

"If nothing else, I'm good at listening."

"Oh, trust me, you're good at kissing too."

Ty's lips grazed my neck. A shiver spread through me. With painful slowness, his lips made their way along my jaw. Each lingering touch sent a pulse through my body, reaching lower and lower. His eager and gentle lips found mine. I breathed him in—salt from the ocean and smoke from the fire. Water and fire. Opposites. Unchanging. Bound.

I rolled towards him; my body trapped in my sleeping bag.

If I could just have him closer. To feel his heat from head to toe. To feel him.

"Damn sleeping bag," he said as he pulled away.

I laughed, settling my willing body back down to the mattress, breathing deep but not so deep that he'd notice it. But what did it matter if he did? His ragged breaths were evidence he felt the same.

His warmth moved away from me but his arm stayed across my chest. As the minutes passed his arm became heavier and his breathing settled. What was I even doing? These feelings I was having, the need to touch him, were foreign to me. Even when Mitchell and I had started seeing each other I hadn't felt like this. It was all so lacking, not like it was with Tyler. Maybe Mitchell and I both found convenience together. Convenience that lacked powerful things like passion.

This thing I felt for Tyler couldn't be real. Real feelings don't manifest in a few days. This was just the surface like when rust forms. It starts with a chemical reaction, oxidisation. These feelings manifested because we were exposed to each other. If we separated now, nothing more would happen. The chemical process would end.

I willed sleep to take hold of me. Expressing myself, allowing unbridled feelings to run free, was dangerous. Or was it? My controlled life with Mitchell hadn't turned out as planned. Maybe I needed to let myself go to feel something true, pure. Something absolute.

Sleep finally took me to its peaceful depths.

MY CHEST FELT LIGHT, heaviness had been lifted. The air around me was warm, so warm it was like I was in a pleasant, comfortable cocoon. Swishing beside me. Maybe fabric? I didn't want to open my eyes to see what it was. Opening my eyes would mean leaving the slice of heaven I'd fallen into. More swishing, and a groan. I opened one eye. Tyler was beside me, stretching. When he moved, the material of the sleeping bag swished.

"Good morning," he said, giving me one of his lopsided smiles.

"Morning."

Was I supposed to give him a good morning kiss? That would be weird. It wasn't like we were at that stage of our relationship. No stop. There was no relationship. Two kisses didn't constitute anything close to a relationship, just a chemical reaction. I needed to stop overthinking everything, every single thought and feeling I had. If it didn't feel right to give him a good morning kiss then I wouldn't.

"The guys said they wanted to go fishing this morning. Do you want to come?"

"No thanks. I'm good. I think I'll just grab a book and enjoy the sun."

He nodded and unzipped his sleeping bag. He sat up and stretched, his t-shirt rising and exposing skin, before he stood up. I let out a breath. Have mercy on me. He had a hard on and his sleep shorts left little to the imagination. I should close my eyes. If I didn't, I wouldn't be able to stop looking. And if I didn't stop looking the tightness between my legs would only get worse. I bit my bottom lip and looked away. Chemical reaction. Oxidisation. Not Tyler's dick. Or the size of it. He needed to leave. Now.

The granting of my wish was good and bad. When he unzipped the door and went to step out his silhouette left me breathless. He wasn't naked, but he didn't need to be. My mind made up all the parts that couldn't be seen—muscles, tanned skin, toned butt. What had happened to not staring? That noble thought was gone. When he turned to smile at me before stepping out, I could nearly hear my lady parts calling out to him.

I sat up and willed my dirty thoughts away. I needed to get outside so I didn't jump his bones when he came back. I grabbed a hoodie and stepped out into the sunshine. Manny and Harrison were already dressed. Nicki and Rosanna sat in their chairs wearing identical PJs to mine—Girl Power cartoons.

"I see you all match," Manny said, looking between us.

"Rosanna's idea. Solidarity, and all that," Nicki said, taking a sip from her water bottle.

"We wore these in high school, twelve years ago, the fun old days," Rosanna said.

"Tyler said you're going fishing," I said to Manny and Harrison as I took a seat next to Rosanna. I was not getting dragged into a conversation about the good old days. Sometimes I felt like I was still there with all the teenagers I dealt with.

"Hopefully we can catch something for lunch," Manny said.

Tyler walked back into the campsite.

"Probably not. Tyler can't catch anything." Harrison gestured to Tyler, then he and Manny smiled at each other. I'm sure there was a double meaning there. I was lucky to notice seeing as my eyes were practically glued to Tyler.

"Ha ha. Aren't you two full of humour," he said, taking the chair opposite me.

"Just stating facts," Manny said. "You've been on a drought for..."

"Just about forever," Harrison finished for him.

Tyler ignored them. "I'm going to get changed."

He walked back to the tent.

Rosanna leant over and whispered, "He's not a piece of meat."

"Oh no, he's much better than that. He's *her* piece of meat," Nicki said, leaning over Rosanna. She was so loud I don't even know why she bothered leaning across.

My face heated. When I saw Manny and Harrison grinning at each other I thought the skin might burn right off my face.

"You people are ridiculous."

"Are we though?" Nicki said, sitting back.

"The way I see it, you two can't keep your eyes off each other," Manny said.

"Well, you see wrong." I stared right at him. "I'm looking at you now."

"As if that counts. Tyler isn't here for you to ogle," Rosanna said.

Why did the conversation have to turn to me and Tyler? They all seemed to get great pleasure discussing us. I sighed. It's because every time they did, I bit their hook like it was baited with...Tyler. Just then he walked out of the tent. Distraction achieved.

Hints of cooking bacon filled the air. My mouth watered... for the bacon. I stood up and looked down at Rosanna and Nicki. "I'm going for breakfast. Are you coming?"

"Sure are," Nicki said, standing up and folding her chair. "The bacon smells divine."

We all walked to the main campsite, chairs in hand. I led the way so they couldn't manipulate Tyler and me into walking together. It wasn't that I didn't want to walk with him, I just didn't need them all making comments about us. My stomach rumbled as we approached. Bacon, sausages and eggs sat in trays.

"Lovers. Lovers." That damn bird had spotted us. "Did you show him ya tits? Have some nooky nooky?" He stared at Tyler and me and then went back to drinking what looked like a cup of tea.

Frank laughed. I ignored him and his stupid bird. Paying no attention to everyone's stares, I added my chair to the circle. Nicki and Rosanna were going to leave a space for Tyler next to me but he ushered them along. I breathed a sigh of relief. I didn't want to give that bird any more ammunition. I had to give Tyler credit; he was thoughtful and I needed to remember to thank him for it later. Maybe with a kiss. Or not.

I went to plait my hair but Tyler's hawk eyes made me stop. He didn't miss a thing. Did he recognise it was a thing I did for comfort?

Frank stood up. "OK troops, after breakfast we're going to head out to the rocks to do some fishing. If you want to join us, be back here at nine. Make sure you're wearing sturdy shoes."

Manny, Harrison and Tyler spoke amongst themselves.

"Are you going fishing?" I asked Nicki and Rosanna.

"I'm going to stay. I'll keep you company," Rosanna said.

"You don't need to stay on my account," I said.

"I'm not really interested in fishing."

"I'm going to give it a go," Nicki said.

It didn't surprise me. She was always willing to try something new. I could step out of my comfort zone but getting hooks out of dying fish was not something I was interested in doing. I'd choose something else to be more adventurous about.

CHAPTER SIXTEEN

Tyler

THE FOUR OF us were ready to leave camp. Rosanna and Mak each had a towel and book ready to hit the beach to read. I was disappointed Mak wasn't joining us. As we walked past them, I paused. I leant in to give her a kiss. My lips embraced hers, once, twice, tasting as much as I dared. She tasted good, like bacon and the sweet taste of Makayla.

I wanted her to know that although I was leaving there was a promise of my return and more kissing to come. Could all that be conveyed in one kiss?

"Enjoy your book," I said as her eyes met mine.

"Thanks." She gave me a small smile. Her complete attention was on me, like no one else existed. I wanted another kiss but that would be overkill. I walked away. I don't know what possessed me to kiss her. Sure, I'd kissed plenty of women before. But nothing like that. Nothing meaningful.

The people making the footsteps behind me were silent. I knew each of them would have something to say but not one of them uttered a word. Not until we hopped into the four-wheel drive.

"What was that?" Manny asked from the front seat.

"What was what?"

"Don't be difficult. That kiss."

Nicki who sat next to me turned her face to mine, as did Harrison beside her.

"It was a kiss. No big deal."

"Since when do you and Mak kiss?" Nicki stared at me like she was trying to decipher unexpected results from an experiment.

"Since we decided it was a fun thing to do."

"In all the years I've known you, I have never seen you kiss someone like that," Harrison said.

"Time to try something new."

Nicki sat back and stared straight ahead. She clutched her hands in her lap. Then she looked at me again. "I hope you're not playing her. Mak spent ten years with the wrong person. I don't want to see her hurt because you think she's a good experiment, or just something frivolous and fun."

"That's not what I meant."

"What did you mean then?"

"Mak's different to anyone I've ever met."

"We're all different to anyone you've ever met."

Jeez she was a hard task master. I thought she was all for this with the way she and Rosanna acted. Maybe they were all for it until there was risk of Makayla getting hurt. A kiss wasn't a promise of forever or even ten years. We weren't putting our hearts out there, just our lips. Of course, it was just our lips...

I needed to show Nicki what I meant about Makayla being different.

"She can be so distant one moment, stubborn to a fault. And then she loses control. Something comes out and I see a glimpse of the person hiding beneath." Were these words actually coming out of me? I sounded love struck...but I was nothing of the sort.

Everyone was silent. How could I explain to them all how drawn I was to her? It was stupid. Feelings were stupid. What I felt made no sense. She made me feel...altered.

"I told her about Clarissa."

Nicki went to say something but Harrison knocked her leg with his. Manny stared at me, concentrating so hard I thought he was trying to read my thoughts.

"About Clarissa?" he asked, his voice doubtful.

"All of it. How sick she was. How it felt when they took her away."

Manny continued to stare at me.

Harrison whispered to Nicki, "Clarissa is Ty's twin sister. He never speaks about her outside our circle."

What Harrison said wasn't quite correct. I would often speak about Clarissa and would even mention her illness sometimes. Just not about how I felt when they took her away. Why did I hold it back? It didn't make sense when I was so willing to share everything else. I think it was the betrayal I felt in that moment. Not by Clarissa, but my own mother. How she made me feel like it was my fault. How I blamed myself.

"And what did Makayla say?" Manny said.

"Nothing."

Manny faced the front. Nicki and Harrison were silent beside me. Manny twisted back to me; a frown set on his face.

"You told her something you've kept deep inside you for years and she said *nothing*?"

"She didn't need to. She let me speak, unguarded." Her silence gave me strength.

Manny didn't say anything. Then he smiled and faced the front again. Nicki reached over and squeezed my leg and held on. "You break her heart and I'll break your bones. I'll weaken them first with sulfuric acid…" She nodded as if satisfied with the plan forming in her mind. Scientists were scary. She was scary.

I was more worried about Makayla breaking my heart. But really, it's not like I had put my heart on the line. Telling Mak about Clarissa didn't constitute matters of the heart. It was just me letting it out, talking to someone. And if she had been with her ex for ten years, I was probably just a rebound. Someone to help her get over him.

OUR CAMPSITE WAS empty when we got back. We carried our catch to the main camp so it could be cooked up for lunch. On the way I could hear Rosanna's throaty laughter coming from one of the other campsites. I glanced over, hoping Mak was with her, but she wasn't.

My shoulders dropped. Rosanna waved us over.

She pointed to the large fish I was holding. "You did good."

"We should get a decent feed from what we caught."

"Mak will be happy. She likes fresh fish." She gave me a coy smile.

"Where is she?"

"She went for a walk that way." She pointed to the left. "Wanted to find a peaceful spot to read."

I nodded and looked in the direction she pointed. I couldn't see her. How far had she gone? "I'll go let her know we're back."

"I doubt that's all you're going to do," Harrison said as I handed the fish to him.

I kicked off my thongs, ignoring the looks they were all giving each other. They couldn't be any more obvious if they tried.

The white sand was hot under my feet. Sand dunes with low vegetation hugged the beach. The light blue water stretched on, hardly a ripple in its surface. Mak sat in the distance, just a small indistinct spot. As I got closer, I saw that she was sitting cross legged with a book in her lap. She wasn't reading it. Her eyes were focused on the water. As I approached, she gave me a smile. My heart lifted.

"How'd the fishing go?"

"We caught a few trevally. Enough for a good lunch." I sat next to her. "What are you reading?"

She showed me the cover. *City of Bones*. "It's YA fantasy. I remember reading it years ago."

"Clarissa has the series."

"Clarissa has good taste."

"Yeah, she likes me."

Mak laughed. "You're her brother."

"It still counts. You have good taste too, you like me."

A grin spread across her face. "Who said I like you?"

"Well, you kissed me."

She placed the book down beside her. "If I remember correctly, it was you who kissed me."

"You kissed me first."

"I didn't mean to."

"And yet, you did."

She stood up. Her face twisted as she tried to suppress her smile and failed. "You can't prove it."

I stood. "I don't need to. We both know the truth. You can't resist me."

Our bodies were so close I wouldn't need to reach far to pull her near and claim her lips once again.

"Can't resist you? I can barely tolerate you."

"Is that so?" I grabbed her waist and pulled her against me. "Tolerate this then."

My mouth collided against hers, and hers opened in an instant. Unrestrained energy burst through my cells. I pulled her closer, harder. I needed to feel every inch of her against me. Her arms encircled my neck. That simple movement brought us closer again, her breasts pushing against my chest. Our mouths moved in unison. Her body, her mouth, I couldn't get enough. When she slipped her tongue in, a tremor spread through me. I moaned. My dick was hard but the rest of me felt like jelly.

CHAPTER SEVENTEEN

Makayla

Heat travelled through me as Ty's erection pressed against me. Everything, all of me, ached for him. I needed him. I wanted him. I couldn't. We shouldn't.

My hands made their way under his shirt and drifted down, over his chest and his stomach. I fingered the raised scar and he shivered at my touch. My heart raced. He moaned again as my hand traced the hair below his belly button. I didn't need to touch myself to know my panties were wet. Slipping my hand into his shorts, I wrapped my fingers around his dick. Ty's moan manifested into a growl.

He ripped his lips away from mine, his breathing ragged. "Fuck Makayla," he half whispered, half moaned.

My hand moved up and down his whole length. I imagined he was inside me. My legs clamped together as the ache between them intensified. I found a rhythm. Faster. Faster again. Never loosening my grip. He thrust in my hand. The breathing in my ear stopped. I didn't. His dick pulsated, and a guttural moan escaped his lips as he came in his shorts. My hand slackened but it didn't stop and his shaking breath matched his legs. Ty rested his head against mine, his breathing slowing when my hand stopped.

I'd never made anyone cum with a hand job before. Never. I stepped away and gave him a tentative smile.

"I think I can tolerate that just fine," he said.

I nodded. That's all I could manage. The whole thing had me out of whack. We were in a public place, alright maybe not that public seeing as I hadn't seen another soul for hours, but public just the same. And I'd lost control of myself and got lost in him. I'd touched a man I barely knew. Not just touched, but had a sexual encounter with him.

I needed to cool down. Wash the excitement from my bikini bottoms. I couldn't even look at him. Him. Tyler. The man who must have been so attracted to me he came in my hand. A man I'd only known a few days.

"I'm going for a swim," I said. "I need to cool off." I didn't want him to think I was trying to get away from him. That he had done something wrong. I tore my tank top and shorts off and went to the water. I didn't even wait for his response.

I walked in, letting the water encircle me inch by inch. I relished in the coolness as the water rose over my skin and my body's temperature adjusted. I focused on relaxing, and recentering my wild thoughts.

"Mak, are you OK?"

I jumped at Tyler's voice. He was right next to me. I nodded. I needed to tell him what I was feeling. He needed to know the crazy he was mixed up in. I needed to give him a chance to run for his life. This was fucked. My mind was fucked. This was not a big deal. It wasn't. People have holiday romances all the time. A mere holiday romance meant he didn't need to know about my crazy.

Just because it happened quickly it didn't mean anything. It was society that put labels on such things—they'd call it a fling or say how shallow it was or how shallow I was. How many times had I told my students that labels didn't matter? It was you, your thoughts, your feelings that mattered. It was what you believed about yourself that mattered. Take a label, screw it up and throw it away. Just because they gave it to you, you didn't have to live it.

"I'm OK." Was I speaking to myself or Tyler? It didn't matter. "I'm OK."

I bent my legs and sat back into the water until I was up to my neck. Tyler moved in front of me and sat, entwining his legs with mine. We both sat there, treading water with our hands, keeping our heads afloat. I made eye contact with him. As always, his expression was open and patient.

"I freaked myself out." My voice was soft as if I was trying to keep the conversation only between the two of us. It was stupid when we were the only two people in sight, but saying it louder would be like admitting my failures to the world.

"What freaked you out?"

"Everything. Like giving someone I barely know a hand job."

"It was a very good hand job, I must say." He reached out and gave my leg a rub. It felt like he was saying it was OK to talk. My heart opened to him a little bit more.

"I've never done that before."

His eyes widened. I studied the surface of the water.

"I mean, made someone cum like that."

"And that freaked you out?"

"No. The fact that I lost control with you freaked me out. The fact I hardly know you freaked me out. The fact that I feel things when I'm with you freaks me out."

"What sort of things?"

"I don't know...things."

I could feel him looking at me. I raised my eyes to his.

"Feelings. You make me feel angry, frustrated, wanted, trusted." They were all scary feelings to have, unsafe feelings, especially the last two.

"And you didn't feel these things with your ex?"

"No." I looked past him to the wide expanse of the water. "I don't know how to explain it. When I'd lost my scholarship, it was because I lost control. I vowed not to do that again. After that I had a plan and stuck to it."

For over ten years I'd stuck to it.

"When I started seeing Mitchell he fitted perfectly into that plan. I just remained on this steady path. I did everything as expected. Feeling, spontaneity, they had no place."

I thought it was a good life. I had my dream of domestic bliss and everything I did was leading to that.

"Were you happy?"

Tyler's hazel eyes were intense as he waited, like he was watching the doors of my mind open. There was no point hiding from the truth or hiding the truth from him. "I thought I was. But the more I'm away from Mitchell the more I realise I was the perfect asset for him...until I wasn't."

"What do you mean?"

"I fit the mould perfectly. An obedient, diligent partner who was there to bolster his standing when required."

Tyler's eyebrows drew together.

I needed to start at the beginning. "When I first met Mitchell, I was in my first year at uni. The loss of the scholarship was a big blow and I was trying to come to terms with my life taking a different path. Mitchell was charming, complimentary. He made me feel special. I clung onto that.

"Then he started in real estate, working his way up, always trying to find the next big deal. By the time he started attracting bigger clients I was working as a counsellor. He pulled me out whenever he needed to boost his credibility. You know, the partner who had a social conscience and helped others. At first, I was proud he thought of me so highly. But I was just fooling myself."

And I'd fooled myself for ten years. I wanted to believe so much that I was blind to the truth. Every time Mitchell put me down or I didn't speak up, I'd fed the lies. And then I was so far in that I just accepted it was the way things were going to be. But that's not what I should have done. Mitchell breaking up with me was a blessing. I couldn't see that before but I could now. I could see a lot of things clearer now.

Tyler's jaw stiffened. It was the only tell I'd found that showed he was not happy. "If you were my partner, I'd be pulling you out at every opportunity."

My stomach fluttered. There were those damn feelings again.

"I don't want you to stop feeling, Mak. I want you to embrace your feelings, even the scary ones. They make life full."

What was he talking about? He was always so collected.

"Do you feel those feelings?"

"Yes, but when I'm with you they're next level." He grabbed my legs and pulled me to him so I was practically sitting in his lap. "And I don't want them to stop."

He kissed me. Not passionately like before but with a quietness and purity that claimed my soul.

CHAPTER EIGHTEEN

Tyler

"Lovers. Lovers. Here come the lovers," Cock Monster squawked as we approached. And with that sort of greeting, it was no wonder everyone sitting around the campsite turned around. Mak attempted to pull her hand from mine but I didn't let go. I gave it a squeeze and it relaxed. Manny's sharp eyes flicked to our hands but he didn't say anything.

"There's still some food left," Rosanna said, pointing to the table. We grabbed some lunch and sat with our friends. The fish was great, cold but great.

Frank stood up. "This afternoon will be free time for you all. We can take people out to do some more fishing or to visit the blowholes. If you prefer you can stay at camp and have a swim."

I glanced over at Mak wondering what she'd prefer to do. Seeing her in a bikini again was on top of my list.

"What do you guys want to do?' Manny asked.

"Swimming sounds good," Nicki said.

Yes, three cheers from me. We headed back to our campsite.

"After that we can play *Cards Against Humanity*. I brought it with me," Rosanna said.

Manny looked over at Harrison. He nodded.

"I'm easy," I said.

"And I'm sure Mak will do what you're doing," Nicki said, giving Mak a nudge.

Mak glared at Nicki. "I do have a mind of my own, you know. You didn't see me tag along to fish just so I could be with Tyler."

Where had that even come from? I'm sure Nicki was only joking.

"Defensive much," Rosanna said.

As we walked back to our campsite, Rosanna narrowed her eyes and studied us, like she should have been the scientist and not Nicki. She didn't try to hide her stare; her eyes wandered up and down and her mouth twisted in thought. What was she seeing? Our hair? It may have been dry but it still had the distinct look of someone who had been swimming in the sea. Or had she noticed how close we had been sitting together? She smiled a sheepish smile and looked away. "Maybe we should play truth or dare instead."

"We're not teenagers," Nicki said.

We'd arrived back at our campsite.

"Maybe some of us are and some of us—" Rosanna tilted her head towards us.

"You're just jealous," I said.

"What, of not having sex in the sand? Who wants sand in all those places?" She indicated to between her legs.

"Mak, do you have any sand in those places?" I asked, mimicking Rosanna's hand movements.

I was sure Mak would be beet red but she just grinned at me. "Are you referring to my vagina?"

Rosanna's mouth snapped shut. I laughed.

"No, I don't believe I have sand in my vagina."

"Me either."

"You don't have a vagina," Harrison said.

"Are you sure?"

"I've seen your junk. No vagina there." A wicked grin appeared. "I'm sure Mak can vouch for that."

Mak blushed and moved away. That girl was no good at keeping secrets. This time Nicki and Rosanna studied us. I tried to act like I didn't notice but couldn't help sneaking looks at them. Mak busied herself with setting up the chairs in a circle.

"By the look on Makayla's face, she's seen your junk too and is embarrassed for you." Harrison plopped down in one of the chairs.

When I sat next to Mak she leaned across and whispered in my ear, "You have nothing to be embarrassed about."

I swung my head around and kissed her with enough passion as I dared in front of a group of people.

When we parted, she said, "You didn't let me finish. I was going to add that lots of men have small dicks." She gave me a kiss on the cheek and turned back to the group.

She'll be wishing it was small later.

I CLOSED the tent after Makayla stepped in.

"How about we open the sleeping bags up? We can put one on the bottom and the other one over us."

"Sure." Mak helped me make the bed before stepping over to her overnight bag to get changed. She folded her clothes and put them on top her bag. I smiled. Would her case be as neat by the end of the holiday? I wanted to tell her not to bother putting on her PJs but that would be presumptuous. After how she'd reacted on the beach earlier, I didn't want to push my luck. I needed to take this at a pace she was comfortable with.

We lay down together. It was like when we first shared a bed—far apart, not touching, every part of me rigid. This was stupid. Last night I'd slept with my arm around her. Today she'd had her hand around my dick.

"So, you think my dick is small?"

She laughed a hearty laugh I'd never get tired of hearing, except when she was laughing about my dick. Did she really think that? My stomach tightened. She shuffled closer so we touched from shoulder to shin. She took hold of my hand.

"Depends on the size of your hand, I guess." There was laughter in her voice.

"And in your hand?"

"Big." She said it with so much conviction my stomach released. She straddled me, her heat penetrating her clothing, her pussy pushing onto my instantly hard dick. As she leant forward, the pressure changed, like she was stroking me. Her warm breath against my ear sent me harder. "Do you know what to do with it though?"

Fuck me. She sat up, rubbing herself against me. A giggle escaped. "Mmm, I suppose it's big enough."

Who was this woman? When I'd told her I didn't want

117

her to stop feeling, that I wanted her to embrace all the feelings, I hadn't expected this. If only there was light in this tent so I could see her, all of her. I reached up and lifted her top off. Her breasts were a silhouette. A flashback of her in a bikini was all I needed to see them in my mind. I caressed each one and then rolled my thumb around her nipple. Mak groaned and sank further onto me, grinding.

I bucked beneath her. There was no way I was cumming in my pants. I pulled her down towards me and then rolled on top of her. There was too much material between us. I knelt back and gripped my shirt. The cotton was soft in my fingers. I yanked it off. Mak shimmied her PJ bottoms and underwear down. I helped her get them off before I did the same to mine.

I lay on top of her, my dick pressing against her thighs. She opened her legs, the heat inviting me in. Not yet. I wanted to drive her to the edge and then push her over. I wanted to see her lose control at my touch. I rubbed my dick against her. It moved easily in her slickness. She was wet for me and I loved it.

I whispered in her ear, "I'm going to make you scream."

Her breath caught and she thrust against me.

"Not so fast. That will be the second orgasm you have tonight." My lips crashed into hers and they moved deliberate and rhythmic. She sighed into my mouth and my body pressed against hers. My dick could have easily slipped in and my promise would have been over before it had even started.

I kissed her jawline, her neck, her collar bone. Then her breasts, one after the other, taking each nipple into my mouth sucking and twirling. Her breathlessness drove me on.

CHAPTER NINETEEN

Makayla

Ty's HAND drifted down my stomach and lower until his fingers found themselves in my wet folds. A finger found my entrance and circled it before plunging in and circling inside. Heat flashed through me. I opened my legs wider, wanting more of him touching me. His finger circled again. I clutched at the sleeping bag beneath me and planted my feet.

His finger slowed and my breathing resumed. My back straightened out and my muscles released. Was it over? His promise of two orgasms...He pulled his finger out and rubbed my hard clit. Holy shit. The tremors started in my legs. My palms flattened out against the sleeping bag. Every bit of energy met between my legs, pulsating. I cried out as waves of pleasure overtook me. Ty pushed his fingers in and I fell apart. Tremor after tremor pushed white hot pleasure through my body. He pulled his fingers out and I lay there, spent, trying to breathe.

Quietness engulfed us. I remembered where we were.

Our friends were only metres away, nothing separated us but air and canvas.

"Do you think they heard me?" I asked.

Ty chuckled. "There's a fair chance."

He reached across me like he was grabbing something. Crinkling in his hand. I raised myself on my elbows to see what he was doing.

"Condom," he said.

"Pretty sure of yourself, aren't you?"

"I wasn't sure of anything. I let you lead the way." He knelt beside me. "You were a bit eager." There was a smile in his voice.

"Still am." I lay back down and Ty settled himself on top of me.

"Ready for your second orgasm of the night?"

"Still sure of yourself, I see."

Would he really be able to do it? I'd never orgasmed during sex before. I was good at faking it though. He didn't answer. Instead, he pushed himself inside of me. Holy crap. I sucked a breath in and gripped his shoulders as he made his way gradually in.

"Still think it's small?" he asked.

I let my breath out to answer. "No."

"Right answer."

He moved in and out lubricating his dick. I could feel him every inch of the way. Every. Single. Inch. As his thrusts sped up, I still gripped his shoulders. That one action helped me stay present.

Ty's lips met mine and he kissed me once, twice. He groaned as his thrusts intensified.

"Stop kissing," I said in desperation. "I can't...Holy crap."

His heavy weight pushed me down or maybe I was pulling him down. As my hips met his, thrust for thrust, I was about to come undone again. Again. Like twice in one night, again. Slow down. He needed to slow down. I needed to enjoy it for longer. I couldn't. Holy shit. I held on tight for the ride. My hips stopped as I clenched around his dick and cried out. Fast. Hard. His breath hitched and his cry matched mine. His hot breath against my neck spread tingles through me as he slowed down.

"That was amazing," I said.

"You're amazing."

Ty rolled off me still breathing hard. The cool night air hit my sweaty body giving me a chill. I searched for my top and underwear. My arms moved as if they were connected to someone else's body. Ty moved beside me, taking the condom off, I guessed. I dressed myself and found the sleeping bag at the bottom of the mattress.

"Thank you," I said as Ty lay beside me.

"Thank *you*." He placed a kiss on top of my head. "I'm never going to get tired of having sex with you."

Was that some kind of pledge?

"TIME TO GET UP LOVE BIRDS." Manny banged on the side of the tent.

My arm and leg were flung over Ty. I rolled over, taking them with me. Ty pushed himself onto his elbow and smiled down at me. That man was way too spritely for this hour of the morning. "We have time for a quickie."

"No, you don't," Manny said from outside the tent.

"I think we do," Ty whispered.

I shook my head. He gave me a peck on the lips. "Just kidding. We don't need Manny listening from our doorway."

Ty stood up and stretched. His hard on stuck out just like it had the day before. He needed to put that damn thing away. It was a risk to my determination. As he put his t-shirt on, I closed my eyes and sighed in relief. He unzipped the door and stepped out.

"We don't need to be standing in your doorway. We could hear you loud and clear from our tents," Manny said.

Great. I should have known they'd have something to say. I stood up and made sure my PJs were on straight. I didn't need to give them any more ammunition. Walking out of the tent, I studied the group in front of me. They were a smug lot.

Harrison smirked as soon as he saw me. "Nicki, what was that thing you said Mak was going to do? Explode?" His hands raised up in an exploding motion.

Rosanna giggled. "Twice."

I went and stood beside Ty and he put his arm across my shoulders. He planted a kiss on top of my head. "It sounds like they enjoyed the show," he said.

I couldn't look at them. The show was pretty darn good and I'd forgotten to turn the volume down.

TY'S PHONE beeped as we closed in on Exmouth. He glanced at the screen and sat up straight before opening the message. I looked too.

Read your email from MTS.

Ty opened his emails. I clenched my teeth. This was a typical Mitchell move. Work was always more important.

"Sorry, I've just got to reply to this email."

I nodded and looked out the window. He was typing for the next twenty minutes. When we arrived at the hotel, he stayed seated while everyone around us started making their way out. The bus had nearly emptied when he finally put his phone back in his pocket.

"Problem?" Manny asked as we disembarked.

Ty nodded. "An investor was concerned about the new technology they're investing in."

"Did you sort it?"

"I think so. I'll see what they come back with."

Ty put his arm around my shoulder and pulled me close for a kiss. His touch spread tranquillity through me. I leant into him.

"OK, come and grab your bags and room keys," Frank said.

"Thank God for solid walls. At least we won't have to listen to you two get it on," Nicki said before heading over to grab her bag.

"You're just jealous," Ty called after her.

We grabbed our bags and key and made our way to our room. I opened the door and walked in. The room was ultra-modern with light coloured, sleek furniture. Straight ahead of us was a spectacular beach view. I left my suitcase beside the bed and went out onto the terrace. A salty, sea breeze brushed against my skin. This was a luxury I hadn't expected.

"Holy smokes," Ty said. He stood behind me, wrapping me in his arms. "They really splashed out."

I nodded. "I thought the tent right on the beach would be hard to beat."

Ty's phone buzzed. My stomach dropped. He didn't move, just continued to hold me close. I doubt that's what he really wanted to do. The phone must have been burning a hole in his pocket. It was burning one in my heart.

I pulled away from him. "You take that." I forced a smile. "I'm going to go chat with the girls."

"OK." He nodded. "I'll see you at dinner."

I grabbed my phone and walked out without looking back. I was so stupid. Why would I think I would be more important than someone's work? I leant against the wall and closed my eyes. Nausea threatened to engulf me. I wouldn't let this happen again. I wouldn't lose myself because I was trying to hold onto someone. I pushed myself against the wall feeling its hard, unyielding surface. My heart needed to be that unyielding. I needed to be unyielding.

I rattled off a text: *Which room are you in?*

24, Rosanna answered.

I glanced at the room numbers as I walked the corridor. 24 was up the stairs. I followed the arrows until I found their room and knocked at the door.

Rosanna answered and looked beside me. "Where's lover boy?"

I made my way past her and into the room. "Working."

"On that multimillion-dollar deal?" she asked.

I shrugged. "I suppose."

I dropped onto one of the beds. Rosanna and Nicki looked at each other. Nicki sat on the opposite bed and studied me. "I hope you're not comparing Ty to Mitchell."

I shrugged again.

Rosanna was standing beside the bed, hands on hips. I raised my eyebrows at her, challenging her.

"You can't be serious?" Rosanna's stare had me sitting tall. Of course, I was bloody serious. Love, rejection, feeling small were all serious emotions. Truth, honesty, acknowledgement was about as serious as you could get.

"At least Mitchell waited a few months before he showed me work was more important."

"Ty is not Mitchell." Her voice was hard.

"Oh really? Why is he working then?"

Rosanna rolled her eyes at me and looked at Nicki. I transferred my attention to her.

"Let's take a moment to think about Ty and his work. He deals with multi-million-dollar accounts. He has built relationships through trust and respect—"

"Mitchell never did any of those things," Rosanna said.

"Ty has been working on the deal for months. He told us all about it the first night we met."

That was true. He was passionate about his work. That wasn't a bad thing. I mean I was passionate about mine too. But passion and obsession are two different things. I wouldn't put work before someone I loved. I shook my head. It's not like I was in love with Ty or him with me. So why was I so worked up?

I glanced at them both and shrugged.

Rosanna sat next to me and took my hand. "I don't think it's fair to compare Ty to Mitchell because he had to send some emails."

I sighed. "I suppose not."

Nicki leant forward. "I know you're scared. You were with Mitchell for a long time. You focused all your energy on him and your future, and that didn't work out. It's natural to be cautious."

"I don't want to be the only one committed in a...whatever this is."

Rosanna squeezed my hand. "Is it just the email that's bothering you?"

"No. You've heard the guys joke about it. Ty hasn't had a long-term relationship. Maybe he doesn't know what commitment is."

"He is committed to his work, his sister and his friends. It's not like he doesn't have relationships. They just haven't been the romantic kind."

I couldn't deny that. Someone who felt as deeply as Ty did, and who shared his feelings openly, was not someone who was withdrawn or a narcissist. I was just overreacting.

Rosanna jumped up. "You broke the no talking about Mitchell pact. That means a deed must follow"

I grunted. Was she seriously doing this? "You've mentioned him, too. If I have to do a deed, so do you."

She ignored me. "I'm choosing the deed." She was seriously doing this. "You need to talk to Ty about how you feel, how you're feeling at this moment, about his work."

The man was going to think I was insane.

"Come on. Let's go to dinner." Rosanna held her hand out to mine and we walked out of the room together.

Ty, Manny and Harrison were waiting for us at the restaurant door. My heart beat fast as I stretched my fingers out and pressed my hands against my legs. Ty's phone was nowhere in sight. As we got closer Ty broke away from the group to meet me.

"Did you get it all sorted?" I asked.

"Yes. Only because you left. Otherwise, I would have been too distracted." He leant in and gave me a kiss.

My heart squeezed. I took his hand. Tyler was the most wonderful, caring man I'd ever met. I loved him. And there was no point denying it. How could I not love him? It wasn't just how he treated me; it was how he helped me grow into a more confident person. It was how his gentleness encouraged me to express myself and open up.

I was such an idiot. Ty was nothing like Mitchell. I didn't need to confess my petty thoughts to him.

CHAPTER TWENTY

Tyler

IT WAS weird wanting to spend so much time with Makayla. We'd sat side by side for over twelve hours yesterday chatting, napping, holding hands. And we did the same now as the bus made its way to the reef. If we were out in the real world, would I feel the same? Or was this because we were virtually trapped together? I'd always thought spending so much time with someone would be suffocating. I'd seen this closeness happen with other people when they started seeing someone, and I'd never understood it.

But it wasn't suffocating at all. I enjoyed waking up with her in the morning, watching as sleep disappeared from her features. Her laughter made me smile. And every day she was more confident in sharing it. I loved being close to her. My body and brain felt like they had been neglected all my life and now they couldn't get enough of the one thing that made them feel alive. I wasn't stupid. This feeling was sure to wear off. I wouldn't be a shiny new toy forever and then she would drift off.

But would she? She had been with her ex for ten years. Her ex, Mitchell, must have been a piece of work. If I never met him, it would be too soon.

I looked out the window. Red dirt and short shrubs passed by. Low sand dunes spread into the distance. The sand changed colour the further we drove and when we stopped it was pure white.

My mind drifted back to something Harrison had said the day before while we waited for the ladies to arrive for dinner. "It will be weird when we get back home, not going out to dinner every night."

"Except for Ty. He goes out a couple of times a week," Manny said.

"Yeah, right. I meant for the rest of us."

The rest of us included Makayla.

"I only do those things because I live close to work," I answered. And I'm bored. I'd never be bored with Makayla. Why did I keep thinking these things? *With* Makayla? Was there a *with* Makayla?

Frank's voice projected through the bus chasing my thoughts away. "Welcome to Turquoise Bay. Today you are going to experience the best snorkelling in Australia. You will see many species of coral and diverse marine life."

"Ooooh," Cock Monster cooed.

"Stronger swimmers can try the drift snorkel. Others who are not so confident can snorkel inside the bay."

Mak looked at me, her eyes wide. "Are we doing the drift snorkel?"

I nodded. I would have stayed in the bay with her if she wanted to, but I much preferred this option.

Cock Monster hopped onto Frank's shoulder. We followed Frank to the beach and grabbed our snorkelling gear. I would never tire of seeing the startling white sand and clear turquoise water of Western Australia. It was like a beach paradise on steroids. We stripped down to our swimwear.

As we headed to the other end of the beach, Cock Monster called out after us, "Babes in bikinis. Show us ya tits."

I shook my head. "That bird may have been amusing the first couple of times it talked but I wish it would just shut up now."

Manny nodded. "I think everyone feels the same."

We stepped into the water to put our snorkelling gear on. Glancing over at Nicki I saw her spit into the mask, rub it in and then rinse it with water.

"It stops the fogging up," she said.

"I know, but how?"

"When the temperature drops inside, the mask fogs up."

"Like windscreens on a cold day?" Harrison asked.

"Yeah. Exactly. The saliva acts as a surfactant. It stops the condensation and fogging. Water droplets form instead and roll away."

"Cool. I never knew that," I said.

"It's great holidaying with a scientist," Rosanna said, spitting into her mask.

Mak and I waited for everyone else to head to the drift site before we followed. I admired her as we walked. Her skin had tanned to a golden brown over the past couple of days. She wasn't model thin. Not even close. And I was grateful for that: more curves to look at.

"What?" she asked.

I forced my gaze to her face. "Just appreciating your curves."

Mak blushed. "Let's go."

"Doesn't mean I'll stop looking."

She pushed off into the water and I followed. The closer we got to the drift snorkel site the stronger the current. We put our faces into the water and were pulled slowly along into another dimension.

There were so many fish. Standing on shore you had no idea what was out here. Round orange fish, so thin it was surprising the current didn't push them over. They must have abs of steel. Do fish even have abs? I laughed at myself imagining their exercise routine. Mak drew her eyebrows together, considering me. I just smiled and pointed to the black fish with yellow stripes and then others with white stripes. The black was so dense the other colours were a stark contrast. Some other black fish swam past with delicate fluttering fins.

Mak pointed to some little blue fish flitting among the coral. They were almost iridescent. The tips of some coral matched the fish's colour. The coral looked like it was the hair of a mad scientist who had just sent a bolt of electricity through her body.

I tugged on Mak's hand and showed her a spotted ray digging in the sand. It was flat against the surface, flapping its wings, moving sand out like a dog digging a hole, getting deeper and deeper. Was it looking for food? How did it know it was there? Smell maybe? Can you smell under water?

I watched as a reef shark glided through the coral. Its long slender body was propelled by a swish of its tail. It paid no attention to us, as if we were just a part of the ecosystem. Mak's eyes were wide as she watched it come closer and then swim away.

The coral was so diverse. Pink coral that reminded me of star bursts emerged here and there. Mounds of branch coral littered the ocean floor. They could have been mistaken for bones in a serial killer's grave yard.

As we neared the end of the drift snorkel a large turtle drifted past, his eyes wise, knowing. I took one last look back at the wonderland as we swam back to shore. Being on this tour was like a wonderland of experiences and emotions. Mak made me feel things I didn't know were possible. Just seeing her swim beside me was cathartic. But at the same time desire flooded through me. I yearned for her, for her touch, for her smile.

CHAPTER TWENTY-ONE

Makayla

I FOLLOWED Tyler out of the ocean. The droplets of water running down his back glinted in the sun. I appreciated how his wet shorts clung to his arse.

"Oh my god, will you two stop looking at each other like you're at a dessert bar?" Nicki said, clustered with our group of friends, drying themselves.

Tyler turned to me and my stomach flipped. I smiled and shrugged. He grinned. "She's good enough to eat."

What the hell?

"La la la." Manny covered his ears and walked away.

Ty burst out laughing. "That's not what I meant."

"Yeah, sure it isn't buddy." Harrison clapped him on the shoulder. "We will just give you two some alone time."

The others followed Manny.

"Just remember you're on a public beach," Rosanna called over her shoulder. My retort stuck in my throat when I remembered what we'd done on a public beach only a few days before.

"Were you thinking what I was thinking?" Ty asked, smirking.

"Probably." I couldn't help but laugh.

I can't remember the last time I'd smiled or laughed so much. Ty made me feel good about myself. He looked at me like he couldn't get enough of me, all of me. Mitchell would always find a flaw, making me feel self-conscious. What had I been thinking all of those years? A life with Mitchell was no future at all. Could there be a future with Ty? Living in different cities would be hard but it could work. At least we were on the same side of the country.

"What are you thinking?" Ty asked.

"About how happy I am."

"Me too. I don't just want this to be a holiday romance."

I took a deep breath in and released it slowly. Was this real? I'd only known Ty for ten days. I was falling too hard, too fast. I couldn't step further away from my comfort zone if I tried. I had no self-control with him. I said things and did things I would normally consider rash. But I didn't regret them. The way I felt about Tyler didn't allow me to regret one moment.

"Does that scare you?" he asked.

He stood before me, waiting, his heart open, vulnerable. Nothing was hidden with this man. I didn't have to guess how he was feeling or what he was thinking. I needed to be as open with him.

"Yes...in so many ways."

He stepped closer and took my hands. His eye contact didn't falter. "In what ways?"

Be brave. Say what you think. "I'm scared about how much I want you. I'm scared that once we're apart, we won't feel the same. I'm scared of thinking about a future that may never be."

Ty nodded. He reached out and smoothed down my hair. His hand rested on the back of my neck. "I'm scared of those things too. But most of all, I'm scared you'll leave me."

I wasn't the one who would leave. "Why would you think that?"

I waited in the silence. Tyler closed his eyes.

"When Clarissa went away, I believed it was my fault. After that, I was scared to let people too close...I don't know... maybe I felt that I would do the same again or that the pain was too much." His eyes searched mine, almost pleading for me to understand. "I know it doesn't make sense. Clarissa came back, she was better. But..."

My throat constricted. I squeezed his hand. "Your fears were real to you. No one has the right to judge you because of them."

He gave me a small smile.

He deserved to hear the truth from me. I needed to tell him how I'd felt when he was working yesterday. If I wanted us to have a future, I needed to start sharing things I would have once withheld.

"Yesterday, when you were answering those emails, it brought back memories of what life was like with Mitchell." I took a deep breath. My hands went to my hair but I stopped them mid-way. Tyler's eyes narrowed. "I was always last on Mitchell's list. Everything else came before me, including work. I'm scared of life repeating itself, Tyler. I don't want to be last on your list."

"You would never be last on my list, Mak."

I nodded. I wanted to believe that.

"I know they are just words, but I will prove it to you every day. Sometimes, work may take my attention, but it will always return to you."

I needed to believe that with all of my heart.

He bent his head to mine. Him, us, here on the beach, could lead to who knows what. Before our lips touched, I whispered, "We're in public."

He smiled. "I know."

As soon as our lips met, I was lost in him.

CHAPTER TWENTY-TWO

Tyler

"I DON'T KNOW why we couldn't stay at the other hotel," Mak said as we entered the foyer of our hotel in Broome.

"I told you, I wanted our last two nights together on tour to be special."

Everything about the new resort was grand. The foyer was cosy and welcoming, rich wooden floors beneath our feet and fans circling lazily above us. Nothing like the hotel we'd left the tour at, where our room had a tiled floor, dated furniture, and popcorn ceilings. Here, huge indigenous paintings in vibrant colours covered the walls. At the old hotel the paint on the walls was dull. There was no atmosphere.

Our bags were taken from us when we checked in. Then we followed the porter to our room.

"Did she say we have our own private pool?" Mak asked.

"Yes."

"Wow. How much did this place cost, Ty?"

"Not much." Five hundred dollars a night not much.

We walked along raised wooden pathways. The gardens on each side were lush and tropical. A lizard sat on a railing, its head turning as it watched us walk past.

"This place is like paradise," Mak said, her eyes taking everything in.

"Your room, sir."

The porter opened the door for us. Mak entered first. More than one wow escaped her lips. I held the door open for the porter. He nodded and smiled as he passed. I pulled some cash out to tip him on the way out.

"Enjoy your stay, sir."

"I'm sure we will. Thank you."

The room had the same feeling as the main foyer—wooden floors, crisp black and white furnishing muted with grey scattered around the room. I found Mak standing at a mesh sliding door that led out to the private garden and pool. I wrapped my arms around her waist savouring the way she automatically sank into me, like we were two beings melding into one.

"It's beautiful." She covered my hands with hers.

"A beautiful room for a beautiful woman."

She twisted in my arms and wrapped her own around my neck. "And a beautiful man."

She pressed against me. Chest to chest. Lips to lips. Her mouth opened to mine and I explored her warmth with my tongue, slowly, deliberately. I wanted to explore every inch of her with my tongue. I moved my hands across her hips with care and to her butt, pulling her closer. A sigh escaped her as my hard on pressed into her.

Mak's lips parted from mine. I pressed my forehead

against hers. The air from our heavy breathing mingled together.

"Let's go for a swim." She pulled away and lifted her tank top. Inch after inch of smooth skin was revealed. Her top hitched on her boobs but she pulled it free. I couldn't blame it. My hands itched to get stuck on them too.

She kicked off her thongs, then slid her shorts past her hips. The material swished down her legs and fell in a heap at her feet. Her moves were precise and focused. And so was I. I'd seen this much of her before but this felt more intimate. She wore cotton underwear that was so practical, so her. I didn't need satin or lace to entice me. Every inch of me, including my growing dick, wanted her.

Her hands made their way to the clasp on her bra and it came loose. The straps held it up until she slid her fingers beneath them and glided them down her arms. Her breasts were round and ample. Fuck me. My dick pulsed in my shorts. She watched me watching her. She chewed on her bottom lip. Fuck, she was hot. Then she slid her underwear off, revealing every inch of herself to me.

I was mesmerised as she turned and stepped into the pool.

"It's no fun swimming alone," she said over her shoulder.

I stripped down and stepped towards the pool. Mak rolled onto her back. Her long brown hair floated around her. The water licked at her breasts. Even though they had flattened and fallen to the side ever so slightly the water didn't cover them. I walked down the steps and made my way towards her. The moving water lifted her floating body before it fell back again.

"You should float with me," she said. 'It's so peaceful."

"I don't think so." My voice was husky.

I pushed her feet apart and pulled her towards me as I made my way to the ledge behind me. I sat and directed her so she was straddling me. Her thighs pressed against mine. Her breasts floated half in and half out of the water.

"What do you want to do then?" she asked.

"You."

Her fingers rested on my shoulders and slid down my arms. When they reached my hands, she lifted them to her breasts. She squeezed my hands into the softness. "How about I do you?"

Makayla continued to squeeze my hands. It was like she was touching herself through me. Then she rubbed against my dick. It jumped to attention, and she licked her parted lips. Fuck. This was better than my wildest dreams. She was better than my wildest dreams. Mak raised herself up and took my dick in her hand and positioned it before sinking down on me.

"Mak."

No condom. But I couldn't give a shit.

I leant my head against the tiles and held onto her breasts as she moved above me. Mak rested her forearms against my head as she took hold of the ledge to steady herself. Her half-closed eyes, her biting her bottom lip, her groans drove me closer to the edge. My hands moved down to her hips and held onto them, guiding her up and down, faster and faster. It was like my dick was in a suction. Tight. Tight. Up. Down. Tight. Tension built at the pit of my stomach. I wasn't ready. I shifted one hand around so my thumb rubbed her nub. Mak threw her head back, a moan escaped. I kept pumping her, up and down. I still wasn't ready. Not yet. Not until...Mak's legs shook. Then she pulsated around me. I drove into her hard. My thumb maintained contact. She cried out as the tension inside me grew. I exploded. I pulled her down hard as my dick throbbed inside her. I shuddered. Tensed. A primal groan escaped.

And I watched the woman of my dreams as we came together.

CHAPTER TWENTY-THREE

Makayla

"WHAT GIVES?" Manny asked Tyler as we took our seats on the bus.

"I wanted our last two nights together on the tour to be special," Tyler answered.

"Is that code for you wanted uninterrupted sex?" Nicki asked.

"No. It means I wanted to show Mak how much she meant to me."

My insides fluttered. That man sure did know how to make a woman feel good. In more ways than one. Rosanna stuck her fingers in her mouth as if she was gagging.

"The breakfast in bed was divine," I said changing the subject.

"You got room service?" Nicki asked.

I showed her and Rosanna the photo. Eggs, a triple serve of bacon, toast and fresh fruit.

"Maybe we should all go stay there," she said.

"Look at this place," Harrison said, pointing out the window. "I doubt us mere mortals could afford it."

He was right. I wouldn't be able to afford that place on my own. Was this the sort of lifestyle Tyler lived?

"This morning we're heading out on a pearl farm tour," Frank said, interrupting my thoughts. "You'll get to experience the inner workings of this unique industry."

I settled back in my seat watching the scenery go past. It was hard to believe this would be our last day on the tour. It would be weird going back to our normal lives after spending fourteen days on the road.

Normal lives. Ty and I had spoken about our life outside the tour—our work, where we lived, what we did in our spare time. But I'd never thought about how vastly different they were.

Tyler lived in the city. He said there was no point living out in the suburbs when it was just himself. He'd go out every Friday for drinks with people from work. Sometimes more. I lived in a unit in the suburbs, close to the school I worked at. Teachers and staff didn't fraternise on a Friday night or any other night for that matter.

He ate out or had meals prepared for him. He said it was boring cooking for one. I didn't do either of those two things often. School counsellors didn't earn that much, investment bankers did. An investment banker of his calibre probably earnt four times the amount I did.

He'd go to the gym every morning, which explained his to-die-for body. The only gym I'd been in was the one at school, and it wasn't by choice, which accounted for my curvaceous body he said he loved.

Were we too different? I didn't know. Maybe. Probably.

Would he find me boring out there in the real world? I guess we'd find out soon enough.

Or would we? It's not like we'd set out a plan of how we would make it work.

I stared out the window at another glorious landscape rushing by. Red dirt, more vibrant than I'd ever seen, stretched into the distance. The landscape was dotted with trees. As the red dirt changed so did the vegetation. By the time we were surrounded by white sand we were also surrounded by mangroves.

When we arrived, Frank took us to an outdoor seating area where a guide waited for us. If I didn't know we were at a pearl farm I would have thought we were just at another perfect W.A. beach location with mangroves, sand and stunning blue water. The only thing that gave it away were the few buildings, the largest about the size of a two-storey house.

The guide smiled at us; her white teeth bright against her tanned skin. "Good morning all and welcome to our pearl farm. In the late 1800s diving for pearl shells was the biggest industry in Broome. In fact, it was the only industry. Pearl shell was used for cutlery handles, buttons and buckles across the world. By the time the early 1900s arrived, Broome supplied eighty percent of the world's pearl shell."

Imagine that, little old Broome, so far away from any capital city, was a world leader.

"Our divers needed to go deeper and deeper to find the best shells. They wore bulky diving suits and heavy helmets. A large amount of the divers were indentured Japanese. The mortality rate was high."

She held up a helmet for us to look at: basic, round like a pearl, with only a tiny window to look through. How did something so primitive stop a man from drowning? How would you feel having to wear that day after day diving the depths to pay off an impossible debt? I shuddered. These men had died in our waters, their families never seeing them again.

"After World War II plastic was invented and became popular. The requirement for pearl shell declined. A new industry was formed—cultured pearl farms."

Ty leant over to me. "Got to give it to them. They adjusted with the times and look at them now."

I nodded.

"On this farm we have Australian South Sea Cultured Pearls. They are the largest pearls and are the best quality based on lustre. The other pearl we have is the Keshi Pearl. These are unique in their shape, not round but irregular."

We passed around the two different types of pearls. Both were beautiful. One was perfectly round, while the other reminded me of a tiny stone. The Keshi Pearl almost shimmered.

"Natural pearls are rare. Some say only around 1 in 10,000 oysters yields a pearl. This would not make a viable industry. Here on the farm, we have remarkable technicians. They open the oyster shells ever so slightly and implant a small shell bead."

She held up a tiny bead, maybe two millimetres in diameter.

"The imbedding of this foreign object irritates the oyster and it protects itself by secreting layers of nacre around it. A pearl forms. The bigger the oyster, the bigger the seed implanted, the bigger the pearl."

Whoever figured this all out was smart.

"Next we're taking one of our boats into the waters of our farm to see harvesting in action."

Ty and I held hands as we followed everyone to the boat. The whole thing was truly fascinating. I'd never thought of pearls being farmed before, certainly not to this level.

We motored out into the clear water. When the boat stopped, the guide leant over the side with a hook and pulled up a mesh rack which held ten huge oysters, bigger than my hand. She took one out and put the rest back in the water.

"This oyster is at the end of its pearl producing life. I will open it up for you and show you the precious pearl inside."

We watched spellbound as she opened it with deft skill. She passed it around. Sitting in the middle of the shell, surrounded by the internal organs of the oyster, was a perfectly formed pearl.

We headed back to shore and went to the gift shop. I walked around with Nicki and Rosanna, admiring the jewellery but not paying the prices any attention. There was no point when I wouldn't be able to afford any.

Nicki stopped to look at some necklaces. "Have you and Ty discussed what you're going to do when you get home?"

"No."

"No?" Rosanna asked.

"We've both said that we don't want it to end but we haven't said how that's going to happen."

It bothered me that we didn't have a plan. We lived in two different cities. It's not like we could date or hang out. Maybe we were just in dreamland.

"Why don't you bring it up?" Nicki suggested.

"I don't know." I did know.

I looked around. Ty, Manny and Harrison were on the

other side of the shop. Harrison saw me watching them and gave me a smile before saying something to Ty.

"You do know," Rosanna said.

I looked at her and shrugged. If I couldn't be honest with my two best friends, who could I be honest with? "I'm afraid. I'd like a whole bloody action plan in place. But planning didn't work out for me last time."

Rosanna took my hand. "OK. Maybe you don't need a ten-year plan, but discussing it is important."

"I agree. I think it will make you feel more secure," Nicki said.

Or not.

WE SAT side by side in the airport lounge. Nicki's, Rosanna's and my flight was leaving first. Fourteen days was all it had taken for me to fall in love with Ty. Insane. We sat away from the others, our last few moments alone. I held his hand tight. Would this be it? Would he change his mind about us as soon as we were apart?

"I can fly up once a month, maybe more," Ty said.

I breathed a sigh of relief. This was the first piece of a plan.

"I'd prefer every weekend," I said, smiling at him.

"Me too." He leant over to kiss me. Heat spread through me. "I mean who wants to wait a whole month to have mind blowing sex."

I laughed. "Yeah. That's way too much to ask."

"I got you something." He reached into his bag and handed me a box. A beautiful, hand carved wooden box inlaid with mother of pearl. The type that came from the pearl farm. I opened it. Inside, on a gold chain was a golden cage holding a single Keshi pearl.

"Ty, it's beautiful. Thank you."

Our flight was called over the loud speaker. Ty and I sat together, holding hands until the line was full. Nicki and Rosanna stood off to the side waiting for me. I stood and took a deep breath. No more avoiding the inevitable. As soon as I walked away our old lives would take over.

Ty leant in. I expected a kiss but he turned his mouth to my ear instead. "I love you, Makayla."

The words left me dumbfounded as my whole world flipped. He kissed me then in front of the whole airport lounge, claiming my lips, my heart, my whole being.

"I'll see you soon," Ty said.

"I'll call you tonight."

Ty nodded. I walked to my friends.

"What's that?" Nicki asked, pointing to the box.

"A gift." I opened the box for them to look at.

"Do you know how much that cost?" Rosanna said.

I shook my head. She turned her attention to Ty. Manny and Harrison were standing beside him. I kept walking as our line moved forward. Two more people and we would be at the check in.

"How much?" I asked.

"Over a grand, easy. Probably two."

What?

"Boarding pass please," the young air hostess said.

I handed my boarding pass over not really paying attention to her or my pass or anything else. Over a grand? Maybe two? Ty had bought me a gift worth more than a week's pay.

That's crazy. I followed the girls blindly then, remembering at the last moment to turn and wave to Ty.

I sat next to the girls and grabbed my phone and book out of my bag. My phone buzzed.

The necklace represents us. The pearl is not perfect, just like you and me. But together, like the pearl and chain, we are perfect. The cage represents how you hold my heart.

My stomach squeezed. I showed Rosanna.

"Is that man real?" She snatched the phone off me to show Nicki.

"Very real." Every glorious part of him including his heart and mind.

Rosanna handed the phone back. "Don't go all googly eyed."

"I'm not."

I texted back *I love you Ty, with every part of me xox*

The plane started off down the runway and I switched my phone off. No, this was not just a holiday romance.

CHAPTER TWENTY-FOUR

Tyler

"Hi," Mak said as she answered the phone. I smiled to myself; I knew that she'd rather be sleeping in but she made an effort to wake early every morning so we could talk.

"Good morning."

Our morning talks after the gym were the best way to start the day. Well, the best way when we were so far apart.

"How was your work out?"

"Good. I can think of better ways to use my energy though."

She laughed. "Me too."

She had me on speaker and I could hear her moving around her kitchen preparing breakfast. We'd done this every morning for the past two weeks. I'd talk to her on my way up the lift, she'd make her breakfast, I'd make mine and we'd sit down together to eat.

"Have you got a busy day?" she asked.

"Yeah. Flat out. Got meetings all morning. Then Ellie has

scheduled some time in so she can get me 'reacquainted with my workload,' as she calls it."

"You're not reacquainted yet?"

"I haven't had much time to be, but she will get me there." I think what Ellie really meant is that she wanted me to become acquainted with not being so hands on and that we would talk about what I should let go of. Anyone would think I couldn't make my own decisions as vice president. She did have a point though.

"Must be good to have someone you can rely on."

"If I didn't have her, I'd be screwed. She filters calls like a pro."

"How long have you worked together?"

"Long enough for her to know that I was different when I got back. She said she liked me better this way, but wouldn't elaborate when I asked her."

"Oh."

Silence. Maybe she was concentrating on making breakfast.

"What are you up to today?"

Cutlery clinked against crockery. I wondered if it was bacon day. And by bacon day I meant just bacon. Sometimes it was cereal, other times it was porridge and other times it was toast.

"You know—teachers, students. I actually have a couple of meetings with students and parents."

"What type of meetings?"

"About behaviour issues. There are some parents who just don't care. I feel sorry for the kids. Maybe if their parents were a little more involved, they wouldn't be where they are now."

"What about the ones you're meeting with today?"

"They're the good kind. As soon as I mentioned meeting, they were trying to figure out a way to fit it in with work."

"That's good."

"Yeah, it's easier when we're all trying to achieve the same outcome."

Talking about outcomes. "I've booked my flights. Three weeks and we'll see each other in person again."

"Good. I miss you."

"I miss you, too." Now would be a good time to plant the seed. "It would be easier if we lived together."

"Yeah. I suppose."

My stomach dropped. That was not the reaction I was expecting. She didn't even seem remotely interested. I loved the idea of seeing her every day. Of waking up next to her and having breakfast together. I thought she would love the idea too.

I SAT at my desk and spun around to look out the window. Slim skyscrapers with glass frontages towered over squat concrete buildings. The light blue sky was a back drop and muted light filled the spaces between them. Melbourne wasn't heavily polluted but like most cities the air wasn't fresh and crisp. I'd discovered how much more I'd appreciated the view in the last couple of weeks. Everything reminded me of Mak, especially the sun. I even appreciated the height, now, because it helped me feel closer to Mak somehow, like maybe there was less distance or interference between us.

"Ty, are you ready for our meeting?" Ellie asked from behind me.

I swivelled around. She stood in the doorway, smiling at me, notebook in hand. She was dressed impeccably, as usual, in a skirt and shirt. I glanced at her feet. I had no idea how she walked in heels that high. She was totally the opposite of Mak. Mak who was practical all the way down to her underwear.

"Yes. Come in."

She closed the door, strode to my desk and sat in one of the chairs. She thought she was here to catch me up but I had more important things to talk about.

"Do you know that females only represent 10% of employees in investment banking?" I asked her.

She shook her head.

"From a female perspective, why do you think that is?"

She considered me. She put her pen down on top of her notepad and laid her hands flat on top. "One reason is that females may not know the industry exists. At our all-girls school, when we were told about prospective careers, banking wasn't one that was mentioned. And I'd never heard of investment banking until I applied for the PA job."

I nodded. Compared to other industries it was quite new.

"Another reason could be that they see it as male dominated and they think it would be hard to break into."

This is exactly why what Mak does was so important.

"So that means we need to tackle this on two fronts."

"You want to increase female representation?" Her voice was a mixture of surprise and doubt.

"I do. I also want to make sure that our female employee's

salaries are equal to that of their male counterparts. I've heard that's a problem faced by many females."

She smiled and picked up her pen. "I'll ask HR for a list of employees, their position and salary."

"Good. Then I want you to explore mentorships—how they work, how we can get one started, whatever you can find."

"OK." She started jotting notes. "What's the deadline for this?"

"Three weeks."

Her eyes widened.

"I don't need it set up in three weeks, but I want to have a solid plan in place."

Her shoulders relaxed and she smiled. "Oh, we will."

CHAPTER TWENTY-FIVE

Makayla

"I DON'T WANT to meet with my parents. Can't you and me just fix it without them?" the year ten student asked. She'd cut her long brown hair and dyed it blonde. The new style gave her a pixie appearance. School didn't allow make-up but she pushed those boundaries by wearing mascara and a nude lip gloss.

I smiled at her, exhausted. She had pressed every single one of my buttons in the last two weeks. My only reaction was to text Ty every time I'd finished dealing with her.

"We've tried that. It hasn't worked."

"Well, it won't work with them either." She crossed her arms and leant back in the chair.

"Why not?"

"All they want to talk about is my boyfriend and how he's no good for me."

Oh. Now the truth comes out. For the last two weeks she

had mentioned everything else under the sun. She'd blamed everything else for her bad behaviour and not doing assigned work. Never once had I heard anything about a boyfriend.

"Why would they think that?"

She scowled at me and crossed her arms tighter. "Because they're old. Like you."

I held my laughter in and touched Ty's pendant. I wasn't that old.

My desk phone rang and I answered it. The person on the line said, "Mr and Mrs Bray are here."

"Thank you. We're not quite ready for them yet. I'll be out soon."

The student set her jaw firm.

"Why would your parents think your boyfriend isn't good for you?"

She shrugged.

"OK. Let's start at the beginning."

––––––––––––

AN HOUR later I was beyond exhausted, but satisfied. The four of us had a plan which included the boyfriend, and everyone was happy. I hoped Ty's day was easier. And the meeting with Ellie, the PA superstar he couldn't live without, got him *reacquainted*.

I texted him. *Meeting one. Success. Hope your day has been good.*

Nothing.

Nothing by the end of my next meeting. What was he doing that was so important that he couldn't send a simple text?

I looked at my phone a hundred times. I even checked to see if it was on. Had I just gone from one narcissist to another? This was exactly how it was with Mitchell. He started off super attentive and by the end I felt like I was imposing on him if I called or texted.

Nothing by the end of the work day.

I didn't text him. I wasn't going to be that needy person. The one who Mitchell would ridicule me about.

Then a message arrived when I got home.

Good day here. Glad your meeting went well.

And nothing else.

ROSANNA and I sat at Nicki's bench watching her cook.

"How's Ty?" she asked as she softened the onions.

"Good. He's been busy at work."

"But not too busy to speak to the girl with his heart?" Rosanna asked, giving me a nudge.

"No. We usually have breakfast together and talk every night. Except tonight. He knows it's girl's night so he set a dinner meeting."

"Ugh. Can that man do no wrong?" Rosanna said. She was so dramatic it made me laugh.

"Give it time. He is a male after all. He's bound to make one mistake," Nicki said from the stove.

I shifted in my seat. "I do wonder when this honeymoon period will be over and reality will hit." I felt like it had started already. It had only taken two weeks.

"Um, never. You two will be in the honeymoon period for

the rest of your lives," Rosanna said. She smothered a cracker in dip and shoved the whole piece in her mouth.

It was kind of her to say it but I doubted it. I was glad it was the last term of school and I was busy helping students. It helped keep my mind off him but it didn't stop my obsession with the delays in his texts or his distracted voice when he called. The man who was an open page now seemed to be obscuring his feelings and himself. Sometimes I wondered if I was just making it up in my head, imagining things that weren't there, just because I expected it. But I wasn't. I knew what to watch out for now, and I wasn't making it up.

I started to think he might be distracted by Ellie. I'd googled her. I couldn't help myself. She was a stunner. A blonde beauty, all legs and a radiant smile, like a movie star. There was nothing plain about her, and in more than one photo they were together—standing close, smiling and laughing, his hand on her arm. My stomach turned. I needed to change the subject.

"You wouldn't believe who texted me last week," I said.

They both looked at me expectantly.

"Mitchell."

Nicki scowled. "What did he want?"

"Nothing much. Just to say hello, catch up."

It was nice of him but I did wonder why now, after months apart.

"I doubt that's all he wanted," Nicki said, stirring the pasta sauce in the pot.

"He said ten years is a long time to spend with someone and we shouldn't lose touch."

He texted a few times and then his messages went dead.

Just like Ty's were going dead. Dead, like he'd lost interest. Dead.

Nicki's shoulders stiffened. "Did you tell him about Ty?"

I placed my hands flat on the bench and sat up straight. "I don't see what Ty has got to do with Mitchell."

Nicki said nothing.

Rosanna rested her hand on my arm. "You know that saying, a bird in the hand is worth two in the bush?"

I nodded.

"Well, one Ty is worth a thousand Mitchells. Don't risk what you have with Ty for a friendship with Mitchell."

"Rosanna is right."

I pulled my arm away. "We texted. That was it. I'm not interested in getting back with Mitchell."

"Are you interested in making it work with Ty?" Nicki asked. She turned her attention from the pot to me, waiting for my answer.

"Of course."

Why would she even ask that?

"Just checking. Sometimes you sound doubtful. And if we can hear it, you can bet Ty can too."

They certainly weren't holding back on their honesty. How would they even know what I thought? I crossed my arms. Nicki made her way to the bench with our calabrese pasta. The rich tomato sauce laced with hot salami and olives coated the pasta. It looked delicious.

She turned back to the stove to collect her bowl before speaking again. "It's just that you're always wary of his work and are always mentioning the honeymoon period or holiday romance."

"Well, you know, his work has been a number one priority

for a long time. And he's never really been in a committed relationship."

Nicki made her way to the table with her bowl.

"This again?"

I sighed. "You're right. I'm just being stupid."

CHAPTER TWENTY-SIX

Tyler

I LEANT BACK in my office chair and looked out the window. The city of Melbourne was as beautiful as ever. With the sun going down, golden light reflected off the windows of the high-rises surrounding me. It had been a long day and it wasn't over yet. Ellie and I still had to finalise some meeting details for next week.

It had been four weeks since Mak and I had flown home. This morning, I'd wanted to ask Mak if she'd thought about my suggestion of moving down here, but the last time I had she'd shut me down. I didn't want to presume she'd be the one to move, so I had been looking at my options. I couldn't transfer. There was nowhere for me to transfer to. I tried not to think of her reaction. Maybe I'd taken her by surprise. Maybe it was too soon to be talking about it. Maybe...

I cast those thoughts aside and called her.

"Hello." Her warm voice greeted me.

"Hey, Mak. Busy day?"

"Hectic. It's the time of year when students decide their future is ruined or they have no idea what they want to do."

"Sounds intense."

She laughed. "You might deal with millions of dollars but I deal with millions of teenage hormones."

"I think I'll stick to investment banking."

There was a knock at my door.

"Sorry, can you wait a sec?"

"Sure."

I spun my chair around to face my desk. "Come in."

Ellie walked in and glanced at the phone in my hand. "Sorry, Ty. I'll be quick."

"What's up?"

"I can't fit Mr Lutwyche into any timeslots next week. He says he'd rather it be a more casual meeting and wants to do dinner."

I smiled. He always wanted a dinner meeting, and he'd insist on paying saying he didn't want it to look like I was bribing him. "When?"

"Next Friday."

I shook my head. "I fly to Sydney Friday morning." Even that was too long to wait for my liking. It was painful not being with Mak every day.

She nodded. "I know. I just wanted to check what other day suits before I go back to him. Thursday is good with me."

Ellie was the best PA I could ask for. She knew when to leave me alone or when to push a little harder. I usually gave into Mr Lutwyche's requests but not this time. There was no way I was delaying my visit to see Mak.

"Let's try next Thursday then."

Ellie gave me a knowing smile before closing the door.

"Sorry about that," I said into the phone.

"Are you still at work?"

"Yeah. It's been one of those weeks."

"And Ellie too?"

"She's having tomorrow off so she's staying back to get next week sorted."

"That's nice of her." Her voice was tight, almost sarcastic.

It was Ellie's job to stay back and help me when I needed her to. It had nothing to do with her being nice.

"I can't wait to see you," I said.

"Same."

Really? That's all she had for me? We'd be seeing each other in just over a week. I thought she'd be more enthusiastic that that. Maybe as we got closer to the day, she'd be more excited.

"How are Nicki and Rosanna?"

"Is Ellie going to dinner with you?"

"Mr Lutwyche always insists she come along."

"Right."

"How are Nicki and Rosanna?"

"Good."

Silence. Was she tired, distracted or just not interested? I should ask. I should find out why she seemed more and more distant every day. Instead, I say, "Well, I better go. Still got work to do."

Chicken shit.

"OK. Bye."

I put the phone down and closed my eyes. When had I become the one that hid their feelings? Was I trying to fight for something that wasn't there? Maybe she'd realised that I was just a rebound and was weighing it all up. I shook my head. I'd finally found the woman of my dreams—funny, complex, real, hot—and it was going down the shitter.

One week. I'd see her again in one week and all would be OK. I just wish it would be here already.

TWO MORE DAYS. The mentoring program was taking form. I was going to use the program to not only increase diversity in our firm but I wanted to share the success within the industry and encourage others to follow. Not telling Mak about it was hard work. Every time I had a little success or came up with a new idea, she was the first person I wanted to share it with.

I plugged my phone into the car and called her as I made my way out of the work carpark. I was running late for dinner with Clarissa, Manny and Harrison. I got distracted with time when I got caught up in work. One thing would lead to another and then it would be later than I thought. It would be OK. Clarissa always made sure I was on my way before putting the food in the oven. Sometimes she would even text to remind me it was our weekly dinner date day.

Mak's phone rang out.

I wound my way through the city streets. When I got out of the chaos, I called Mak again.

"Hello." Her voice was tight. Bad day maybe?

"Hey. How's your day been?"

"Fine."

She was dismissive. I gripped the steering wheel as I pulled up at a red light.

"I'm busy, Ty. I'm heading to a staff dinner."

I didn't remember her telling me about dinner.

"Sorry, I didn't realise."

"Distracted by work again?"

The light changed to green and I took off slowly. I took a breath in.

"I've been really busy."

"I know. You're always busy. With work."

What on earth? This couldn't wait. I'd been skirting around the subject and her attitude for days. It was time to talk.

I looked for a carpark to turn into. Nothing. I turned into a side street and parked.

"Mak, what's going on?"

"I'm sick of being second, Ty. You love your work and that's great. Everyone should love their job."

"When have I put you second?" My voice mirrored my grip on the steering wheel.

"When don't you?"

"I ring every day."

"Like it's a chore."

"It's not a chore, Mak. I call you because I want to. Because I miss you."

"I'm busy. I've got to go."

I turned the car off.

"I'm busy too, but this isn't something we can ignore. I don't want to wait until I'm there to sort this out."

She grunted. A door slammed. "Why bother?"

What the hell had gotten into her?

"What?"

"Why bother? It was a holiday romance. Probably the longest romance you've been committed to."

"I beg your pardon?" I planted my feet firm on the floor. Every part of me was stiff.

"You heard me."

"Don't be fucking ridiculous. If I wasn't committed, why would I be taking time off work to fly to Sydney to see you?"

"I have an idea. Don't. Stay there with your precious job and your perfect PA."

"At least she's not as fucking crazy as you."

My ears throbbed to the beat of my hammering heart.

"Good bye, Tyler."

And that was it, she was gone.

CHAPTER TWENTY-SEVEN

Makayla

THURSDAY NIGHT. Girl's night. I wished I could just miss it. Bit hard when the dinner was at my house. The doorbell rang and my stomach dropped. As soon as the door opened Nicki and Rosanna came bustling in.

Nicki handed me a gift bag. "For your dirty weekend."

I took it from her but didn't look inside.

"What time is Ty getting here?" Rosanna asked.

They threw their bags on the couch and made their way to the kitchen.

"Have you changed your sheets? Fresh sheets are the best sex sheets," Nicki said.

Rosanna laughed. "What's the point? They won't stay clean."

"True. Especially with a double O morning, noon and night."

I poured them some wine and filled mine to the top. I handed them their glasses and turned my attention to the wine bottle, studying the pretty flower pattern petal by petal, biding my time. The conversation about Tyler was inevitable but avoiding it for as long as I could was a calculated, if not flawed, strategy.

Rosanna looked around the kitchen. "Where's dinner?"

"I've ordered Indian." I took a swig of my drink and another one, preparing for the avalanche.

"Since when do you order in?" Nicki asked.

"Maybe she's conserving her energy."

I emptied my glass, refilled it and took a deep breath in. "Ty's not coming."

Nicki's head whipped towards me. "What?"

"I told him not to bother."

"What? Why?" Rosanna set her glass down.

"It wasn't working." I turned away from them and got some cutlery and bowls out.

"It wasn't working, how?" Rosanna asked.

"He was more interested in his job." And spending time with his PA.

"He was taking time off work to visit you." Rosanna's voice was a mixture of surprise and sarcasm.

"Do we need to talk about it? It's over. That's it."

"But you were so happy," Nicki said.

I took my time setting the table, not making eye contact with either of them. "It was good while it lasted, like a virus invading a cell and then being repelled."

"You're referring to Ty as a virus?" Nicki said.

The doorbell rang, relieving me from answering. If I had been going to answer, I'd have said yes. A virus that knew how to invade my weak heart. It had spread through my whole body, even my brain, making me think that someone could like me just the way I was. That complicated me, who still hadn't figured myself out, could just be accepted and loved. That I could be someone's absolute.

What I wanted to say to them was that I was relieved. Relieved that I'd rejected the virus before it had absorbed all of me. But what part hadn't it absorbed? Tyler had made me feel as light as a kite in the wind. But the lead he injected with a few words brought me back to earth with a quick thump. Reality sucked. And it hurt.

I gave the delivery guy a tip and wished that I had ordered copious amounts of wine as well. Or gin. Or anything alcoholic, except vodka. It was going to be a long dinner. I didn't want to talk about Ty. His work. Ellie. Being second best. The better option would be to binge watch Supernatural and get lost in killing monsters while the words 'at least she's not as fucking crazy as you' echoed in my mind.

Drink more wine.

IF I THOUGHT a month without seeing Ty was slow, a week without talking to him was torture. No texts during the day. No phone calls in the morning or at night. My mind would drift to him and then I'd chastise myself.

I was already on season three of *Supernatural*. The monsters I needed to kill were the ones inside me. Regret. Jealousy. Melancholy. Uncertainty. And the biggest of all, insecurity. That was the one that led to all the others. They were the monsters I couldn't kill.

My phone beeped. My heart jumped.

Mitchell.

He'd been texting on and off.

Hey there. How're things going?

Good. Well as good as could be expected.

Want to catch up for dinner tomorrow night?

Did I? I guess it was better than...nothing?

OK

Excellent. Meet me at the grill at six.

I put the phone down. Seeing Mitchell again would be nice, I guess. I didn't miss him anymore. I missed the thought of him. No, not even that. The fact that we'd spent ten years together wasn't something we should reject or ignore. Nicki and Rosanna could say what they like, but Mitchell still held a part of me, of my history. Maybe they thought I'd fall back under his spell. I wouldn't. I was a different person now.

Dinner would be enjoyable. There didn't need to be any more to it.

MITCHELL WAS WAITING for me at the bar, his blonde hair sitting perfectly. He leant back against the bar surveying his surroundings. He studied each person and group. He hadn't noticed me enter and I took the chance to scrutinise him. What I would have once considered a confident stance I now recognised as arrogance, superiority, like he was keeping an eye on his minions. He was the total opposite of Ty who never judged anyone, not even me...until those words left his lips.

"Hi, Mitchell," I said as I approached him.

"Makayla, how are you?"

"Good. You?"

"You look drawn."

Strike one. Thanks Mitchell, way to make a girl feel good. I reached up to smooth down my hair and stopped myself. I didn't need comfort. "Busy time of year."

"Tell me about it. Everyone wants to move their properties. As the silly season hits people are eager to move into their new homes."

I nodded and signalled to the bartender. Mitchell didn't even turn to acknowledge his presence. Ty would have been on a first name basis with him. He believed everyone deserved respect and should be appreciated no matter what service they provided. Not only that, he wouldn't have said 'you look drawn', he would have actually asked if I was OK.

"The firm has really stepped it up in the last few months, taking on more top end buyers. I'm in discussions now about partnership level," Mitchell said, drawing my attention back to him.

"That's great." I accepted my drink from the bartender and took some big sips.

"I've got a great penthouse on the books at the moment. The owners have a few more properties they're thinking of putting on the market. They want to retire to the Hunter Valley."

Maybe catching up wasn't such a great idea. It wasn't really catching up. It was more like the Mitchell monologue show. The only thing he'd said about me was his little put down.

"Here they are now."

What? Here who were?

"George. Brad. Great to see you."

Mitchell looked at me. I put my drink down and stepped forward.

Strike two.

"This is Makayla. She'll be joining us."

I reached out my hand. George came straight in for a kiss. Brad was more reserved and shook my hand instead. I glanced sideways at Mitchell. Why was I even surprised that he'd set me up like this?

"Mitchell says you're looking at moving to the Hunter?" I said.

George smiled and his grey bushy eyebrows joined in on the happiness. "We've dreamed of it for years. The area is green, divine."

Mitchell smiled. "I've got a table booked. Let's head in."

I went to follow but George put his hand on my arm. "Don't forget your drink."

"Thank you."

I caught Mitchell's hard stare as I turned back to get my drink. I didn't bother taking it with me. I drowned it in one gulp and left the glass on the bar.

George waited for me so we could enter together. Mitchell had got us the best table, overlooking the river. The same table we always dined at with clients. He pulled out a chair for me. I smiled and sat. I knew the drill. I was here to fill a part, to speak only when addressed or if I had something Mitchell deemed important enough for me to contribute. Taking a deep breath, I gritted my teeth.

The waiter approached for our drinks order. Mitchell indicated to the guests of honour.

Brad looked over at me. "Please take Makayla's order first."

"I'll have a Moscow Mule please."

The waiter nodded. Brad and George looked at each other, a hint of a smile on their lips. I imagined Mitchell's inner scowl. He would have wanted me to be proper and order wine.

"We'll have one of those, too, please," Brad said. He ran his hand over his non-existent hair. "We fell in love over Moscow Mules."

A half smile reached my lips. "So did I."

Brad glanced at Mitchell as he went to order. I waited; my breath held. One. Two. Three. Would he do it? Would he lower himself? "One for me too, please."

I should have known an impression was more important to him.

"We were in Singapore. Both at a conference," George said.

"What about you?" Brad asked us both.

Mitchell opened his mouth to answer.

"I was in Perth," I answered before the lie could leave his mouth. Mitchell clamped his lips shut. He'd never been to Perth. Or been in love. He rested his arm on top of my chair. A subtle warning.

"What conference were you at?" I asked.

"Bio medical science," Brad replied. Light glinted off his well-tanned head. "George was a pharmaceutical rep. I was a medical director."

"And you'd never crossed paths before?"

"Funny, isn't it?"

I nodded. My fingers touched Ty's pendant. Fate worked when you least expected it. When you were trying to figure yourself out it brought you people like Ty. People who wanted you to just be yourself. Until your insecurities led you into acting...crazy.

"My friend works for an investment bank. One of his perspectives is for medical research. It's really interesting."

Mitchell's hand pressed closer.

"What sort of research?" Brad asked, his brown eyes watching me keenly.

I harnessed my inner Ty. "Emotion regulation in young people, starting at age five. Studies have shown this is an increasing problem in society." I gauged their reaction. They were both watching me. "The research company has developed a program which can detect when children are using different types of digital technology to regulate their emotions and can determine if that technology has become ineffective."

"That will be a game changer." Brad let out a low whistle. "It could reduce aggression, self-harm, and alcohol and drug abuse."

"They need to fund continued research to show the program is effective. They want to install the program onto the phones and tablets of a sample group and monitor results for two years."

Brad nodded.

The waiter came with our drinks. Brad and George raised their glasses. Mitchell and I did the same.

"To falling in love," George said.

To falling in love. I was such an idiot. I'd let my insecurities drive away the man I loved. I'd let my insecurities ruin my best chance of happiness. Insecurities Mitchell helped nurture.

The waiter came back for our food order. As Brad and

George placed their order Mitchell angry whispered to me, "What are you doing?"

"Talking to your guests. Isn't that why I'm here?"

"No. You're here to listen and support me."

Strike three.

I drew a breath in. And another. As soon as I placed my order, I addressed Brad and George, "Would you please excuse us for a moment?"

They nodded. Mitchell followed me out to the bar.

Before I could say a word, he spat out, "They're here to talk real estate, not some pie in the sky bullshit."

"Not everything is about you, Mitchell."

"I didn't invite you so you could steal their attention."

I braced my body and mind. "I'm not your lap dog, Mitchell. For ten years I catered to your whims. Not anymore."

His mouth fell open.

"You have said nothing nice to me since I arrived. You never say anything nice to me." I faced him straight on.

"Oh, come on." He threw his hands up in the air.

"Go on, turn it back onto me. That's what you always do. It won't work. I won't believe there is something wrong with me." Confidence and firmness filled my tone. Two things I'd never displayed around Mitchell before. Two things Tyler would never discourage.

He stared at me, wide-eyed.

"You're the person with the problem here," I said.

"I am not." Pouting was so unflattering.

I was not going to put up with his bullshit anymore. I deserved better than what he had to give. I thought maybe we could be friends, but he's not the type of person to have friends unless they can do something for him. Mitchell would no longer be a part of my future.

"I'm going back in there now to have dinner with two gentlemen who seem genuine and kind. I will not shut up like you want me to. I will not give you all the glory like you want me to."

I stalked off before he could answer.

"Everything OK?" George asked, his warm brown eyes studying me.

"Never better." Well, mostly. In this moment anyway. Out there, when I leave, the world had turned to shit.

He nodded as Mitchell took his seat.

"We'd like the number of that friend of yours. I think that research is something we'd like to invest in."

I nodded, then recited Ty's number off the top of my head. "Don't tell him I sent you."

"You don't want him to know?"

I shook my head. "He's the man I fell in love with over Moscow Mules."

CHAPTER TWENTY-EIGHT

Tyler

"AT WHAT POINT in time did you think it was a good idea to call Makayla crazy?" Clarissa asked. Her brown hair was tied in a messy bun at the top of her head, wisps of it falling out creating an almost halo look. Her hazel eyes bored into me. She chopped the vegetables like she was chopping off someone's head. My head.

It had taken a week for me to front up for dinner. During that time, I could barely function. I couldn't concentrate without thinking of Mak and replaying the argument over in my mind. I'd read *Diary of a Wombat* more than once to try to lift my deflated spirits. But not even that wombat and her crazy antics could help me. Clarissa, Manny and Harrison would text me and I'd reply with one or two-word answers. I hadn't told them what had happened, just that it had.

It was one of the worst weeks of my life. I'd see something funny and want to text Mak only to remember I couldn't anymore. Not that I needed reminding. I lost count of the times Ellie would come into my office and find me staring out the window. I'd wait for the calls from Mak telling me about her day, her laughing or telling me about something she'd read but the calls never came. Emptiness was all I was left with.

"Ty, at what point in time did you think it was a good idea to call Makayla crazy?" Clarissa repeated. She stopped chopping and stared at me.

"I don't know. She was just..."

Manny laughed.

I turned on him. "Do you think this is funny?"

He shook his head and waved his hand up and down at me. "This? No. The fact that for the first time in who knows how long, you lost control and it led you to this—" he indicated to me again "—is quite amusing."

I scowled. The *this* he was referring to was my scruffiness. My unshaved face. My loose tracksuit pants.

Harrison chuckled.

"Tyler." Clarissa's frustrated voice demanded my attention.

I shrugged my shoulders. "I don't know... I should have spoken to her as soon as I realised she was pulling away."

"Why didn't you?'

"I was afraid that she'd tell me straight out that she didn't love me and she was leaving."

I could have solved the problem by being open like usual but instead I'd held my feelings back. And the more I thought about it the more I should have known what the problem was. She had once been brave enough to tell me her fears. She'd learnt to speak without concern. I kicked myself knowing that she was no longer confident enough to do that and that I'd failed her.

Clarissa smacked the knife against the board. I turned my attention back to her. "What are you going to do about it?"

"Nothing,"

"What?"

"How am I supposed to come back from this? It's a royal fuck up." I sighed. "I fucked up."

Harrison stood beside me and placed a hand on my shoulder. "Ty, she loves you. You love her. You can find a way."

"So, you've got these two morons teasing you about not being the relationship kind. You've got Makayla who's given ten years of her life to the wrong person," Clarissa said.

Commitment. The lack of it. Makayla had said it loud and clear.

"Then there's you. You have held onto our childhood trauma. My illness. My being taken away. Mum leaving. You've held onto it like a shield to protect you from being hurt."

"With good reason."

And she was right. I was scared of being committed. I wasn't scared of the commitment itself but being left. And Mak had done exactly that.

Clarissa closed her eyes. I smiled as I imagined her visualising stabbing me in the head.

"OK. OK. I get it. She was scared too. She pushed me away to protect herself."

My phone rang. It was a number I didn't recognise.

"Don't you dare answer that," Clarissa said.

I ignored her and walked away.

"Tyler speaking."

"Hello, Tyler. My name is Brad McGregor. My partner

George and I would like to speak to you about an investment opportunity we've heard you are offering."

How did they get my private number?

"Sure. Would you like to book a meeting for Monday to discuss the perspective you're interested in?"

"Yes, please. It's the emotion regulation technology."

My passion project. My heart skipped a beat. We needed another investor or two to get the full funding we required.

"I'd be happy to walk you through that opportunity."

"Excellent."

I put him on speaker so I could look at my calendar.

"We learnt about it from a lovely young lady while we shared Moscow Mules together."

The drink I would forever associate with Makayla. Another fragment of my heart disintegrated.

Whispers in the background. Someone chastising him.

"My partner and I mentioned how we fell in love over Moscow Mules."

This was weird.

"Then she told us how she fell in love with you the same way."

Tingles spread through me. I'd fallen in love with someone the same way.

"Makayla?"

"Yes."

"I'll get my PA to call you on Monday to set up a meeting." I needed to get off the phone.

"Wonderful."

I walked back into the kitchen.

"I need a plan."

CHAPTER TWENTY-NINE

Makayla

"I DON'T REALLY THINK a road trip is going to help," I said.

Nicki ignored me and started picking clothes up off the floor, checking if they were clean and throwing them into a bag. She raised her eyebrows more than once at the state of my room—clothes strewn everywhere, drawers half open, books stacked on my bedside table.

It was 6 a.m. on Saturday. Normal people, unlike Ty, the early riser, were still in bed. I would have been too if she hadn't woken me up. I'd probably have stayed in bed half the day if given the chance. In bed, I didn't have to face the real world. The world that Tyler was no longer a part of.

"I've got a lot planned this weekend." I started pulling things out of the bag.

"Like what?"

Like staying in my pyjamas and watching another season of *Supernatural*. Like thinking how stupid I was for letting my insecurities push the man I loved away. Like thinking about how much I missed said man.

"Like *things*."

"Rosanna will be here in fifteen minutes. I suggest you shower."

I rolled my eyes and walked away. I wasn't going to win this argument. When I got out of the bathroom, Nicki was sitting on my bed next to my packed bag. Heaven only knew what she'd packed. I didn't really care. Hopefully, it was just leggings, t-shirts and sensible underwear.

"I'll let you get dressed. Don't forget your toiletries."

I walked back into the bathroom to pack my toiletry bag. If I didn't do it now, I'd forget. I was forgetting a lot of things lately. Except Ty, he crept into my thoughts multiple times a day. My phone didn't light up with random messages from him. I missed falling asleep talking to him. Sometimes when he'd had a big day at work, he'd call me on the way home. He always ended the call by saying how just talking to me made him feel better.

And I'd accused him of not being committed. He was right. I was acting crazy.

I chucked my toiletries in my bag and shoved things around so they could fit. Dropping the towel, I threw some comfy clothes on. I had no idea where we were going but I may as well be comfortable getting there. Nicki was in the middle of texting when I came out to the lounge.

"Ready?"

"I suppose. Let me grab some snacks."

Nicki followed me to the kitchen and watched as I collected chocolate, bags of lollies and chips. She opened the cupboards and stared. "What the hell, Mak? When was the last time you ate a proper meal?"

I shrugged. I followed her out to the car and put my bag in the boot. I knew the last time. But to say it out loud...

"Last week, when I had dinner with Mitchell," I said as I hopped into the back seat.

"What?" Nicki said, her blonde head whipping around to me in the back seat.

"The last time I ate a proper meal was with Mitchell."

"You had dinner with Mitchell?" Rosanna asked as she pulled away from the curb.

"I thought he wanted to catch up, say hi, see what we'd been up to."

"And?" Rosanna prompted.

"And he didn't. I was there to perform a task."

Nicki's jaw clenched. "Arsehole."

I gave her a small smile and sunk into the back seat when she faced the front. I stared out at the brick houses with their green lawns and brick fences as we drove by. Everything out there was the same as it always was, but I wasn't. I wasn't the same as I always was.

"Nothing had changed. He was passive aggressive, putting me down in his own special way."

Rosanna gripped the steering wheel.

"So, I told him I wasn't going to be his lap dog. He didn't like it. But I didn't care."

Rosanna reached back and squeezed my leg.

"And for two weeks I've thought about how my insecurities ruined the best thing I had."

"Ty," Nicki said.

"Have you tried ringing him?" Rosanna asked.

"What would I say? Sorry I didn't trust you? I'm an idiot? Will you forgive me?"

Nicki and Rosanna glanced at each other.

"All of the above," Nicki said.

I shook my head. "I can't. I can't ask for his forgiveness when I don't deserve it."

And I didn't. I'd asked for commitment and hadn't been able to deliver the same in return. The first hurdle we encountered and I ran like the speed of the wind at Steep Point.

I didn't even know why I was jealous. It didn't make sense. Ty had done nothing to make me think that that he preferred Ellie or her company. He'd never spoken about her in any other capacity other than work. Even when he spoke to her while I was on the phone it was just his every day voice, nothing suspicious about it. Stupid freaking insecurities.

I pressed my hands against my cheeks and willed myself not to cry. I mean, seriously how much could one person cry? Sometimes I wondered what I was actually crying for. Was it because of the failed relationship or because I was the one who'd failed in the relationship? Tyler was a good person. A kind person. An honest person. I'd recognised that the first day I'd met him. Then why didn't I believe in him enough? It wasn't him at all. It was me. I didn't believe I was good enough to be loved.

I shook my head and stared out the window. Tears rolled down my cheeks.

THE CAR BRAKED and I woke up. I looked at my watch: 3 p.m. We'd been driving for hours. Ridiculous for a weekend trip. We'd get there, spend the night and then have to return.

We were no longer on the highway. The signs pointed to Cape Byron. We'd driven all this way to look at a lighthouse? Rosanna parked the car. I got out and stretched. I was stiff after sitting for hours. Nicki was still in the car, busy texting. She gave me a smile and hopped out.

"Ready?" Rosanna asked her.

"Sure am."

We made our way to the path, Rosanna and Nicki in the lead.

"Check out the view," Rosanna said, her black hair glinting in the sun.

Deep blue water stretched below us as far as the eyes could see, framed by a long beach on one side. I soaked up the sun and peacefulness, and let calm settle inside me.

"Would you ladies like a photo?" a passerby asked,

"Yes please," Nicki handed over her phone.

I smiled, allowing myself to be happy in the moment. And why wouldn't I be happy? I was in a beautiful part of Australia with my two best friends. My heart may have been sad but it was also grateful. I'd make the most of this trip because they'd done this for me.

We continued up the path, the railing on one side and the road on the other. The lighthouse came into view, towering above us, high on the point. Its stark white walls contrasted against the blue sky and a few scattered clouds; I went to the stairs so I could get closer. I wanted to feel its power and see its beauty up close. Lighthouses had fascinated me as a child. Every lighthouse had its own colour scheme and pattern on the tower so that mariners could tell them apart during the day, and its own unique flash patterns at night. These features allowed mariners to know where they were.

My shoulders dropped as I realised these were the types of random facts I'd share with Ty. He never seemed bored with them. Or me. He accepted me for who I was—the strange things I'd say, the way I was learning to be myself, how I didn't dress like a model, how I didn't even look like a model. I pressed my hand against his pendant. Isn't that what you want from someone you love? For them to love you as you are?

I stared up at the lighthouse. The Cape Byron Lighthouse was not very tall, probably because it sat so high up on the headland. It had a boxy building at its base and the traditional cylindrical tower. I strolled around the building studying it.

"Mak, we're going this way," Rosanna said.

I nodded and followed.

CHAPTER THIRTY

Tyler

I sᴛᴏᴏᴅ next to the railing. The ocean stretched to the horizon, blue against blue. I wiped my sweaty palms against my shorts while shifting from foot to foot and watching the path.

"Will you relax?" Manny said. "You're making me nervous."

I looked behind me and to the ocean below. Why had I decided to stand so close to the edge when we were so high up? Maybe the two fears were competing against each other—falling to my death or rejection by Mak. One was definitely worse than the other.

I saw Nicki first. Her blonde curls. Then Rosanna and her jet-black hair. When I spotted Mak my heart flew to my throat. The smile that often adorned her face was nowhere to be seen. Her long brown hair fell flat and had lost its persistent shine. She was as beautiful as ever, but broken, like the broken pottery the Japanese would repair with gold. I hoped with everything that I could be her gold.

"Breathe," Harrison said beside me.

I nodded and took a couple of breaths. Mak didn't see me; her eyes were locked on the view. I'd rehearsed what I was going to say a hundred times but couldn't remember one word.

I approached Mak. She moved aside as if she was expecting me to pass. I took a deep breath and wiped my hands. "Mak."

Makayla turned to me and her eyes opened wide the moment she recognised me. My hands twitched; I held them still even though all I wanted to do was touch her.

"Would you like to take a photo with me?" I pointed to the sign stating we were at the most easterly point of the Australian mainland. "We could pretend to be a happy couple."

She just stared at me. Tears rolled down her cheeks. That was not what I'd been expecting. Our friends were no help, they just stood there silent. I stepped in closer, gauging her reaction. When she didn't move away, I wrapped her in my arms. She reached around me. My shirt pulled tight as she clutched it in her hands. I kissed the top of her head. The familiar rose scent of her shampoo calmed me and gave me the strength I needed.

"It's OK, Mak."

What I really wanted to ask was why she was crying but I didn't know if it was a safe question. I mean, she could have hit me. Calling someone crazy could have that effect. Clarissa with a knife or Mak with a fist, they were both dangerous options. Cause and effect.

"I've missed you, Ty. I'm sorry." Her voice was thick with tears.

"I'm sorry too. I'm sorry for—" I had to spit it out "—calling you crazy. I'm sorry for not calling you straight back and for waiting so long."

She pulled away and cupped my cheek with her palm. Her brown eyes searched my face as if making sure I wasn't an apparition. "It wasn't only you who should have done all those things. I should have too." Her face drew close to mine. "I love you, Ty."

"Not as much as I love you."

Her soft lips found mine. Kissing mine was exactly where they were meant to be.

"Lovers, lovers, here come the lovers," Harrison squawked.

"Ooh, nooky nooky," Nicki replied.

They cracked up laughing.

———

MAKAYLA GASPED at the view from the deck of our cabin. The hinterland stretched all the way to the ocean. I stepped up beside her and took her hand.

"You like it?"

"Yes." She faced me. "You don't need to keep spending a fortune on beautiful places. I'd be happy with you anywhere."

"It's worth it to see your face every time."

She pointed to the bath on the deck. "Shall we?"

I grinned at her. "I've got a better idea."

She stepped away from me and raised her eyebrows. "Better than getting naked?"

"No one said anything about *not* getting naked." I stepped

towards her. "You have way too many clothes on for my liking."

"Take them off then."

"Eager much?" It took all of my restraint not to rip her clothes off. I eyed the hammock in the corner. Perfect. I stepped closer, taking her hips and forcing her back a step. I kissed her; my mouth as enthusiastic as my dick. My lips made their way to the spot between her neck and shoulder. She sighed and my heartbeat picked up pace. My hand reached under her top and found her breasts, giving one and then the other a hard squeeze just the way she liked it. Her breath caught. I traced my tongue to her ear and whispered, "Are you wet for me yet?"

"Yes," she whispered.

When my fingers traced down her stomach, she shivered at my touch, which only drove my need for her. I moved her back another step.

"Let's see how wet you are."

I manoeuvred my hand below her waistband and lower still until my fingers were between her legs. Her folds were slick. I glided my fingers backwards and forwards while I guided her back another step. We were only a step away from the hammock now.

I pulled her leggings and underwear down, smiling about their practicality, and helped her step out of them, before sitting her down in the hammock, her legs off the side. I knelt before her and kissed my way up her thighs. Pushing her legs out wider, I tasted her. Her fingers clutched the edge of the hammock.

"You can scream here." My tongue savoured her, moving up, circling, stroking. "And no one will hear you."

MAKAYLA LAY in my arms in the hammock. Sex and sweat filled the air.

"I love you, Mak. I'm sorry for not talking to you when I should have."

She glanced up at me. "What do you mean?"

"When we were on the tour, I loved spending every moment with you. I was sure that you felt the same. In my heart all I wanted was for that to continue."

She nodded. "Me too."

"Then when we got back to our every day lives it wasn't the same. You weren't the same. You were becoming distant and I didn't know why. I thought you had changed your mind."

She wrapped her arm tighter around me. "I'm sorry. It wasn't your fault I was feeling that way. All I could keep thinking is that it was like Mitchell all over again."

"But it *was* my fault, Mak. You had told me your greatest fear and I did nothing to dispel it. So, your fear fed into my fear. When I asked you to move, you shut me down. I didn't ask you why. All I could think was that you realised you didn't love me anymore."

I stilled, waiting for her answer. She took my hand.

"I do love you, Ty. I didn't want to move for someone who was more interested in their work. And who already had the perfect woman by their side."

I pushed her away so I could see her face. "What are you talking about? You're the perfect woman."

"Ellie." She said her name with resignation.

"Ellie?"

"You spend eight plus hours a day with her. She's movie star beautiful. I'm drab and boring compared to her." Mak's eyes searched mine as if trying to find answers.

"She might be talented and the best PA I could ever ask for but she's not you, Mak. She doesn't make me smile like you do. She doesn't get me like you do. I go to sleep thinking of you and wake wanting to see your face."

She sighed. "We were so stupid. We nearly lost each other *because* we were so scared of losing each other and then didn't speak to each other about it."

"Pretty dumb, huh?"

She nodded. "You know how some animals have a partner for life? You're that partner for me. I can't imagine a life without you."

My heart lifted.

"I'll move down after the end of the school year. I don't want to leave the students in limbo."

She rested her head back down and I kissed the top of it. "That sounds like a plan."

"It won't be hard to get a job. There are schools close to your apartment."

That was true. I'd done the research. She must have too.

"We don't have to stay there. We can move wherever you like," I said. "I'll be happy wherever you're happy."

"I'll be happy with you." She snuggled in deeper. "Does it have a hammock? The apartment?"

"It will by the time you get there." I laughed.

"Sounds perfect."

"I've been working on something," I said.

She changed position and looked up at me.

"Well, not just me, Ellie helped. We're setting up a

mentorship for females. It's nearly ready to go. We want to pitch it to schools in the next couple of weeks."

Mak's eyes teared up. "That's a great idea."

"I know it's a bit late in the year and a lot of students have decided their pathway but there may be some that are interested."

She nodded. "There will be."

My heart lifted. "Do you think so?"

"For sure. I'd be interested in anything you pitched."

"How about getting married?"

She stretched up and kissed me. "I'd definitely be interested in that."

EPILOGUE

Makayla

"Are you ready?" Nicki asked, smoothing down the front of my cream lace dress. It was a simple V-neck dress, knee length with a ribbon at the waist.

"I've never been more ready in my life."

Rosanna stood beside us. "You look beautiful."

I took their hands. My best friends for life. The two people I owed everything to, especially this day.

"If it weren't for the two of you, I wouldn't have found the love of my life."

"You can thank us later," Nicki said, giving Rosanna a wink.

I had no idea what she was talking about.

I looked down at my white sneakers. They were the safest way to traverse across the rocks. Rosanna and Nicki wore dresses similar to mine, but in black, with matching sensible shoes. We had planned on taking the beach route but the rising tide prevented that.

We made our way across the rocks, Manny and Harrison meeting us in case we needed help. I had to stop myself from forging ahead. Our friends and the rocky hills slowed me down. I gave the piles of rocks we passed a mere glance.

Tyler was waiting for me beside a sign, wearing black shorts and a blue short-sleeved dress shirt. Giddy warmth spread through me. Clarissa was standing beside him in a dress matching Nicki's and Rosanna's, a baby bump notice-able. Her hair was braided and her wide smile matched his. As soon as I reached him, he took my hands.

I glanced at the sign *You're standing at the northern most point of the Australian continent.*

Tyler and I smiled at each other as Harrison stepped forward and started the ceremony.

"I'm duly authorised to solemnise marriages according to Australian law."

He'd taken the course just so he could marry us in the middle of nowhere. I wanted to hug him right there but I stayed still. I wanted to marry Tyler more.

"I need to remind you your marriage is the union between you both to the exclusion of all others."

"Except us," Manny said.

Harrison grinned at him.

"Yeah, you can't get rid of us," Nicki said. "We have naming rights to your first born."

"At the end of the ceremony you will be bound by the promises you make to each other." Harrison looked at me. I took a deep breath.

"Tyler, I promise to trust in your love and commitment and return it to you."

Tyler squeezed my hands and I looked up into his smiling face.

I continued, "You have embraced every part of me, including my insecurities, and have always encouraged me to feel. I have no fear feeling with you. You are my absolute." I looked around at the scenery surrounding us. Bright blue water stretched to two rocky islands. "For the rest of my days, I want to explore the extremities with you."

Tyler leant in and kissed me. My stomach lifted at his touch and I stepped closer, wanting more.

"Enough already," Nicki said, pulling me away. "We want to hear Ty's vows."

Ty grinned at me. "Makayla, I promise to stay committed to you until the day I die. You make me brave, so brave that I believe in forever."

I believed in forever, too.

"The thought that I'd never find my absolute disappeared the day I met you. I look forward to exploring the ends of the world with you." He leant in and whispered, "And to deliver you a double orgasm wherever we go."

"We can hear you," Manny said.

Rosanna giggled.

"Told you that you could thank us later," Nicki said.

I rolled my eyes.

"Rings," Harrison said.

Clarissa handed them to us.

I slid the ring onto Tyler's finger. "Tyler, with this ring, I thee wed."

"Makayla, this ring holds every promise I make today and every day afterwards."

As soon as the ring slid onto my finger, he wrapped me in

his arms. I slid my hands under his shirt and pulled him closer. His tongue found mine and I smiled as I tasted vodka and ginger beer.

"Just so you know," Manny said, interrupting us, "We've actually booked you a room tonight." He walked away holding Clarissa's hand.

"There was no way we wanted to listen to the Tyler show," Rosanna said, following him.

"You're just jealous," Tyler called after them.

Harrison sighed. "I pronounce you man and wife."

"Go consummate your marriage," Nicki said. She and Harrison were laughing so hard they were holding their sides. "And as Cock Monster once said, show him ya tits."

THANK YOU for reading my novel.

The next book in the Love Down Under Series is As Busy as a Bee.

To receive a free short story, be notified of future releases, and to keep up to date with other news, please join my newsletter. https://www.subscribepage.com/p9p9yo

---

BOOK REVIEWS from awesome readers like you are the lifeblood of authors, especially new authors. Reviews help readers find new books and authors find new readers. They don't need to be long or detailed, even two sentence reviews add value.

It would be appreciated if you could leave a review here:

Amazon

Goodreads

BookBub

OTHER books available in the Love Down Under Series are:

The Cat's Out of the Bag

She's started a new life. He's escaping his. Can two tortured souls find a future together?

Evie's a survivor. After rebuilding herself and her life, she's feeling the one thing she never thought she would – happy.

Until Jesse...

When she meets Jesse while volunteering at a cat shelter, dark memories of her past return. She is stronger now and wants to trust him, but after all she's been through, is trust even possible?

Jesse's a self-made billionaire yearning to get away from his empty life and the money-hungry parasites who inhabit it.

The plan?

Go to sunny Australia, leaving his old life behind, to find himself. But instead of finding just himself, he finds Evie, who is everything anyone should aspire to be. Now, what he aspires to be, is hers.

But to be hers, he needs to tell her everything and putting his heart on the line is hard.

The quest to find a cat a forever home leads them to travel across the country together. Will they find the strength to confide in each other? Or will the close quarters drive them apart?

Let Sleeping Dogs Lie

When she left him…

…Tara couldn't explain why.

After five years, did she still have feelings for Shepherd?

Her brother's passing hit Tara hard and it left a scar. That night, at the party, when she saw Shepherd high, Tara had no choice, it was over. It brought up too many painful memories and she wouldn't go through it again. The decision was simple.

She had to leave.

No goodbye.

For Shepherd, losing Tara broke his heart. Not knowing why she left, well that pain he addressed with drugs, alcohol, and meaningless relationships. After he hit rock bottom, he cleaned up and came up with a plan to get her back. Could it work?

It was his only shot.

Would a desperate ruse, with the best intentions, but costing a fortune, give him the chance to win her heart for good? Or would it ruin him?

Will she be brave enough to be loved?

**When two opposites collide will their differences
ignite a spark?**

Frankie and Sebastian live totally different lives. Lives that are
entwined through polo, the sport of kings. How entangled will they
become?

Australian farmgirl, Frankie, has no interest in high society or the
rich, arrogant riders she has to deal with, especially Sebastian. Her
heart may be softening to his kindness and love of horses, but her
brain won't be convinced. She's looking forward to her summer
break on the farm, away from him...

...until her parents invite Sebastian to stay.

Sebastian never felt comfortable in his role as the Crown Prince of
Oleander. He'd rather spend his days working with horses, playing
polo and being with Frankie, whose fiery spirit has set his heart
aflame.

But pressure from his mother, the Queen, to return to his royal
duties is mounting. Everything he desires is in danger of being
ripped away.

Can Sebastian convince Frankie that his hopes and dreams aren't so
different from hers, or is he destined to return to a life he doesn't
want, alone?

Down The Rabbit Hole

Love and secrets are a tricky combination

For Emily, going home isn't easy, especially when her small town never felt like home in the first place. She escaped Alma seven years ago when she went to university, but now her estranged father needs her help. At least returning means spending time with the only good thing in town—her best friend, Luke.

Luke always knew Emily needed to be free of their hometown, so he withheld his true feelings. Even though she has returned, he knows she will never stay. He tries hard to respect the boundaries of their friendship but every moment they spend together makes it harder to deny their connection. Self-control dissipates. One kiss turns into two...

But is Luke really the man Emily remembers? When Emily discovers Luke has betrayed her trust, they could lose the most precious thing of all—each other.

As Busy as a Bee

Mixing business with pleasure is a risky affair...

Clare Walker is a third-generation company woman. Hart Apples saved her family from destitution and now it's her turn to return the favour. Work is her one true love, leaving no room for anything – or anyone – else. She knows what the company needs to survive another generation, and it's not the owner's son – sexy, know-it-all, Beau Hart.

Beau is in line to take over the family business. And with that business comes the operations manager from hell - Clare. She's at his throat the moment he walks in. He would find her wit and feistiness attractive if only it wasn't pitted against him.

What they don't know is that Beau's father has elected them as the company's saviours. What will be harder—fighting off their growing attraction or saving the company they both love?

ACKNOWLEDGMENTS

Cover by 100 Covers
Edited by Salt & Sage Books
Proofread by Half Caff Press
And thanks to my amazing beta readers

ABOUT THE AUTHOR

Cynthia is a project officer by day and a writer by night. She enjoys writing about places she visited with her daughter while they travelled around Australia. She says that travel and reading are the best educators. Still, to this day, they both enjoy travelling and reading. A love of animals sees them feature in her books, some have small parts, others larger.

Find her online: http://cynthiaterelst.com/

All of her social links can be found here, Linktree: https://linktr.ee/cynthiaterelst